Dizzy Izzy

Zee 'C'

With love + best
wishes
Zee 'C'

Published by New Generation Publishing in 2017

Front cover photograph courtesy of Beth Hoffman

First Edition

www.newgeneration-publishing.com

New Generation Publishing

This book is dedicated to my family and friends who have supported and encouraged me to continue to transfer my stories from my head onto paper

Dizzy Izzy Leaves Home

The clackety clack of the early morning goods train woke Izzy with a start.

"Oh no" she groaned "I am so tired of that train. It wakes me every morning just as I've got to sleep."

The train rumbled past almost shaking Izzy off her bed. Izzy didn't like sleeping close to the ground and as she was almost grown up now, her parents had allowed her to choose where to sleep. She had chosen this area of the garden as it was furthest from the train track but also the furthest corner away from the house and sometimes the gardener didn't always weed this corner as ruthlessly as the rest of the garden. Izzy, even as a young fairy had always been a dreamer. She had never felt at home in this garden. It was always so formal and clean. It meant there was very little for the fairy family to do as no strange animals or insects visited or passed through this immaculate but uninteresting area.

Despite choosing this private and distant corner Izzy still felt bored and restless and longed to explore the world. Izzy felt sure that there was a better place to live. She wasn't sure exactly what she was looking for but it would certainly be a long way from a train track! Izzy tiredly turned over and attempted to go back to sleep although she knew that peace was an impossible now the thundering of high speed trains passing by had begun.

For the next few weeks Izzy continued to dream of freedom from the ever constant rumbling and clattering of the train from early morning to late at night. As it was summer there were more trains, carrying heavier loads, and less hours of darkness for the fairies to work. Therefore Izzy and her family were engaged continuously in general housekeeping and provision gathering. As the weather was warm and sunny their sleeping hours were hot and sweaty and with such a formal garden, very little shade.

Increasingly Izzy became determined to escape. She knew she would miss her parents, sisters and extended family but was also excited by her daring nature. No other fairy had left the family home in generations. She dreamed of cool shady areas, running water to bathe and swim in, lots of visitors passing through, chaotic intertwined brightly coloured flowers and best of all no trains!

Izzy was so busy dreaming her dream she earned the nickname Dizzy Izzy because she forgot what she was supposed to be doing, half doing the job then drifting off to begin another. The family found themselves forever reminding her what she should be doing, and checking if she had completed her chores. Tempers became frayed and after one particular hot, sultry night Izzy's mother lost her temper completely with Izzy and Izzy retaliated. Izzy flounced off, packed her clean dress in her cobweb bag and flew out of the garden, over the fence in the opposite direction to the train track. Soon Izzy began feeling tired, her wings ached and she felt hungry. As the garden had provided everything the family needed Izzy had never needed to fly far and she was unfit for such a long journey. Izzy decided to rest for a while and fluttered down on to roof of a little house in a garden. No sooner had she landed and folded her wings than a huge snore erupted from beneath her.

She let out a frightened squeal which immediately woke the occupant of the house. With a rattling of chains out of the door bounded the largest animal poor Izzy had ever seen. Throwing its head in the air it let out a deep growl and followed it with a frenzy of barks. Suddenly a bright light was switched on and the sound of a door been unlocked. Poor Izzy, despite feeling tired, jumped to her feet, unfolded her wings and stumbled off the roof. Her wings refused to obey her commands and she found herself tumbling down the back of the little house. The animal tried hard to reach behind his house but couldn't fit between it and the fence. Izzy cowered in the corner shivering with fear. Eventually a human voice shouted,

"Barney, for goodness sake, shut up! What do you think you are doing? You know there is no room behind your kennel so there cannot be anything there. You've been dreaming again. Go back to bed and be quiet, or else the neighbours will be complaining again."

The animal slunk off, suitably chastised, back to bed but Izzy was too tired and scared to move.

Eventually she fell into an uneasy sleep continuously hearing the shuffling, snoring and wheezing of what she realised was a dog. Izzy vowed she would be up and away before this great bumbling animal woke up properly in the morning because she was sure he would sniff her out when he awoke.

Izzy was so tired it was daylight when she woke up and of course fairies cannot move around when humans are up and about as they may see them. Therefore Izzy was confined to her hiding place for the day. All day every so often the dog came to the tiny gap between the kennel and the fence and sniffed, snuffled and tried to scratch a hole to get at Izzy but as it was another hot and sticky day he lacked the energy and motivation to continue his mission. Eventually the long day came to an end, the sun set and the dog crawled into his kennel and fell asleep.

Slowly and quietly Izzy unfolded her wings and stood up. She stretched her legs and wings and then fluttered up out of her hiding place. She flew up and over the fence as quickly as possible before the dog awoke again. Izzy now had a problem she had no idea where she was. Although, at that moment, home and the rattling train beckoned she had lost her sense of direction. Dizzy Izzy was about to embark on her private adventures in her search for her 'perfect' home.

After leaving the 'dog garden' as she had dubbed it she headed away from the houses and out into the country. Unfortunately there were no street lamps here and no visible landmarks. After a while her wings became tired so she fluttered down into an open space. There didn't appear to be any little houses, dog kennels or even fences she could land on. Suddenly she spied a large lump in the middle of the field. Deciding to investigate she fluttered across to it and gently landed on it. Suddenly she felt a rippling effect under her feet and a strange rope rose up and flicked across this warm rock. Alarmed Izzy ran towards the next level away from the swishing rope. Suddenly the higher rock moved and Izzy froze on the spot. She felt warm air emerging from two holes and then an eye appeared. Oh crikey what had Izzy stumbled on now? Was she about to be eaten by a living rock? Why was it warm with rippling waves? Oh help!! Yet again her wings felt like lead and just wouldn't obey her brain to fly away. Suddenly a quiet voice said,

"Are you a fairy? What's your name? Where are you going? Where are the rest of your family? Are you lost?"

The voice was so friendly that Izzy's heart stopped racing quite so fast.

"Yes, I'm a fairy, my name is Izzy, who are you?" Izzy replied.

"My name is Tulip, my mum Daisy is asleep just over there, that black and white cow."

"Oh, are you a baby cow" laughed Izzy "I've never seen a cow before."

"What do you mean you've never seen a cow before?" Tulip asked.

"Well I lived in a garden next to the railway line all my life and I never went outside the fence. We didn't need to as we had enough food and things in the garden."

"Why are you here then?" asked Tulip.

"Well I was tired of the noisy train. The garden didn't need us for anything. No adventures or exciting things happening. Then last night, no hang on the night before, I had a big quarrel with my mum and flew away to find a real garden."

"Well this isn't a garden, it's the middle of a cow field and I haven't seen any houses or gardens around here. There aren't even any flowers except us cows who all have flower names," laughed Tulip.

4

"That is okay, I spent yesterday behind a dog kennel trying to keep out of the dog's mouth so you're a big improvement at least you're friendly, warm and very comfortable. Would you mind if I rested the night out on your back?"

"You're welcome to but it will get a bit cold later on then what happens when morning comes and everyone wakes up? You cannot fly away in daylight and there is nowhere to hide here."

"Oh goodness I never thought about that one Tulip, but I'm so tired my wings just won't work to go any further."

"I know," cried Tulip, "Jump on my nose, make sure you don't tickle it or I'll sneeze and blow you away, and crawl up my face and rest in my ear. You'll be warm, snug and safe even when I get up in the morning."

"You clever thing," exclaimed Izzy, "Ok here goes but it looks a very steep climb up your nose."

"At least give it a try Izzy, I'll keep real still."

Izzy jumped and landed on Tulip's nose, it was wet and warm. Tulip flicked her tongue out and Izzy was horrified how big it was. It was pink and rough when Izzy reached down to touch it. Izzy turned round and looked up the mountain facing her. It was such a long climb up Tulip's face to her ears. It would have been so much easier to fly. Izzy tried to crawl up but it was no good she just couldn't make it.

"It's no good Tulip, I cannot get up there until my wings get rested then I can fly to the top of your head. Where can I spend the night meanwhile?"

"I suppose if I lay my head across my side there would be a warm bed between my face and my side," Tulip replied "Let's try it."

"Ok," Izzy answered.

Gently Tulip moved her head so that Izzy didn't fall off and settled in a comfortable position then Izzy slid off the side of Tulip's nose into the crease. Oh what a lovely warm, cosy, comfortable bed she had found. Tulip's quiet breathing provided a lullaby and Izzy was soon fast asleep.

Suddenly it was morning and the sun was rising on another beautiful day. Izzy stretched, yawned and flew up to the top of Tulip's head and crawled into her ear. Tulip's ear wiggled whilst Izzy got comfortable and secure then Tulip rose slowly to her feet. No one knew Tulip's secret that she had an adorable tiny fairy hiding in her ear all day. She felt so proud. She behaved normally all day but she didn't play with the other calves and didn't move her head quickly in case Izzy fell out.

At sunset the cows settled back to sleep and Izzy crawled out of Tulip's ear. She slid down her head and placed a kiss on her nose.

"Thanks for a great day, you're a special young lady, I'll never forget you but I must be on my way now," Izzy said.

Off Izzy flew. After such a restful night and day and all the exercise she was able to fly much further that night before needing to rest. She looked around her to see where she could shelter for the day. The dawn was breaking so Izzy knew she couldn't go much further. She saw some houses but decided not to venture in that direction in case she stumbled on dogs, cats or humans. Suddenly she spied some big green shapes that looked like great big garages.

Izzy couldn't imagine what might be in such big sheds but because they were so big she felt sure she could find shelter from prying eyes for the day. She flew across and landed on top of the door of the nearest one. Peering through the crack she could just see a strange shape resting inside. She hoped it was not a living thing as big as that! She crawled through the gap at the top and fluttered down to investigate this queer looking object. There were three of them and Izzy thought they looked a bit like flying insects. She shuddered at the thought they might be giant living insects but it was daylight now and she was tired so she hadn't any choice but stay here for the day.

Izzy landed on the top if its head and to her relief found it was a roof and that it was metal underfoot. With a thankful sigh she crawled through a tiny gap and into a dark space. Suddenly she was falling! She tried to fly but was too tired and plumped down on to a soft cushion. She wondered what she had landed on but it was too dark to see she decided to just settle down and go to sleep. At least it was warm but not alive or moving so she felt quite safe.

After a while she was rudely awakened by light flooding into the building from large open doors and the sound of human voices. Izzy had been in such a deep sleep she couldn't function for a while. Suddenly the door to her hiding place began to open. Izzy scrambled off her cushion and slid into a dark corner hoping no one saw her because it was too late to fly away now. A human jumped in and sat down on the very cushion, moments earlier, Izzy had been sleeping on. The person fiddled with some knobs and then Izzy felt a shudder and an engine started.

Oh my goodness now what was happening? She felt the great insect begin to move and suddenly they were out in the sunshine. Izzy risked a quick peek from her hiding place but she couldn't see anything. Dare she crawl out of this dark place and see what was happening? She crawled a little way out and looked up. She could see the back of the person's head. Good, that meant as long as she was careful and they didn't turn their head she was safe. She scrambled out a bit further. Oh the thing was gathering speed. Now it felt as though it was climbing. Izzy couldn't bear it any longer, whether she was spotted or not, she was going to see what was happening.

She found a ledge and jumped on it but still couldn't see out of the window. By now she was more excited than frightened. It felt as though the 'thing', insect or vehicle or whatever it was, was flying but that was impossible. Only fairies, elves, birds and insects could fly and this was none of these. Spying a bit of strap that went across the person's shoulder Izzy deftly leapt on. Oh she could see out of the window now! She was flying in a flying vehicle. She had never flown in daylight before. The sights were fantastic. Izzy became a bit braver and leant a bit closer to the person to get a better view. She suddenly realized that the person was a young woman. Izzy felt safer, women were supposed to be kinder and gentler and accepted unusual happenings. Izzy felt instinctively that the woman would not hurt her if she noticed her. To get a better view of the sights in front, Izzy crawled on to the arm. The woman looked down.

"Oh a fairy, a tiny fairy, travelling with me!" she exclaimed.

"Pardon," a disembodied voice inquired. "What did you say?"

The woman rethought quickly knowing control would not believe her if she said she could see a fairy.

"I was just thinking aloud and remarked it looked like a fairy town," she replied.

"Oh that is aright then," control tower replied "Are you ok?"

"Yes," replied the pilot and flicked a switch quickly.

"Ok why don't you jump on the dashboard and travel in style little fairy. You'll have a better view. I promise I'll tell you when to hide before we get back to base. By the way my name is Penny what's yours?"

Izzy was speechless, fancy a grown up human not only been able to see her, but talking to her as well, as though it was all perfectly normal.

"I'm Izzy," replied Izzy before nimbly hopping on to a ledge right in front of the window. Penny flicked the switch back so she was in radio contact again. Although no words were spoken Izzy thoroughly enjoyed her unexpected ride in the sky, flying without using her energy. Eventually the flight was over. Izzy accepted she must return to her hiding place. Penny brought the plane down on to the runway and ran it back to the outside of the building. As she climbed out she held open her pocket on her flying suit and offered Izzy a safe passage away from the hanger and other humans. Izzy gratefully accepted the offer and the two returned to the office. Without a word Penny silently opened a drawer and indicated for Izzy to hide in there. Not sure what was going to happen next,

Izzy held back for a moment then decided to trust her new friend.

Once Izzy was safely in the drawer Penny took off her flying suit and sat down at the desk to fill in some forms. The door opened and other pilots tramped in. Izzy could hear lots of voices all appearing to be male. Although Izzy was left wondering what was actually happening she instinctively felt certain her new friend would not let anything awful happen to her. Eventually one by one the voices left the office until only 1 male voice was left.

"Are you joining us for a drink then Penny?" he asked

"Not tonight Sean, by the time I've cleared away in here I want to get off as I'm going to do a few days intensive revision before our final exams."

"Oh you spoilsport. You know what they say all work no play etc.!"

"Yes, I know makes Penny a dull girl but this girl is determined to do well. There will plenty of time to play when I've qualified as a pilot."

"Ok, I know. I'm only teasing. Have a good evening see you tomorrow."

"See you tomorrow Sean," replied Penny.

When the door had closed behind Sean, Penny opened the drawer where Izzy was hiding and held out her hand.

"Okay little one, come out and tell me all about yourself. We won't be disturbed now everyone has gone."

Izzy leapt on to the outstretched hand and was transported across to the desk and gently set down on the desk. Spying a convenient seat she sat on it.

"Just a minute. Let me turn it over. It's a pencil sharpener and you may cut yourself on it" Penny explained. Izzy jumped up and allowed Penny to turn over her seat.

"Right tell me your story."

Penny listened with rapt attention as Izzy explained about the noise from the train, the too perfect garden and the argument with her mother. She then went on to tell Penny about the dog and the calf and by the time she had finished Penny was laughing.

"Oh you poor thing. Did you enjoy today's adventure though?"

"Oh yes" breathed Izzy, "it was ace. I'd love to do it again sometime."

"Well you can go with me anytime you want" replied Penny. "In the meantime I've a tiny cottage in the country. Would you like to come with me? Actually the way you describe the house next to the railway line, I think I may know it. Had it yellow walls and white paint, lots of windows?"

"Yes that's right. Oh don't tell me I'll still get shook out of bed with that horrible train."

"Oh, Izzy, no you won't feel or hear the train at the cottage. We are on the other side of the track and it winds away from us. I just meant you could easily go and visit your family if you come to live with me. Also if you want you can sleep in the house. I'm sure we can fashion a bed for you so you are free to come and go as you please," Penny laughed.

Sliding completed forms into the desk drawer Penny picked up her handbag and opened the top. Holding it close to the edge of the desk for Izzy to jump in she said,

"Come on Dizzy Izzy, let's go and see if my quaint little cottage meets with your vision of a dream home. We've got lots of cottage garden flowers providing lots of colour. There is a weeping willow tree whose branches almost touch the ground, a stream running down one side and across the bottom with a rickety garden gate leading to a wood. In the center of the forest there is a clearing, where the bluebells bloom and a small waterfall and pond which on sunny days catch the sunlight. I've occasionally seen fairies and elves riding those sunbeams but they mainly play on the moonbeams. That's why I could see you because I believe in fairies, have done all my life, and always will."

"Now I understand. I thought it was strange as I had always been taught that only some children could see us and grown up people harmed us because they didn't know we were there."

"I'm sure that's true but I seem to be different. I always have been. Fairies and elves are my friends and I hope you will be happy in my garden and make some new friends with the many visitors who live there or pass through."

"Already I'm sure it's going to be great. Did you really mean it that I can also fly with you?"

"Of course I meant it but come on let us go home first and work out how to live together."

"Sounds great lets go then," answered Izzy

Laughing together Penny and Izzy set off to explore Izzy's 'dream world' never mind 'dream home'.

Dizzy Izzy's New Adventure

Penny walked across the car park towards a little sports car. Although not new it was precious to Penny. She unlocked the door and climbed in. Opening her bag she held out her hand to Izzy.

"Do you want to come out and ride on the front dashboard."

"What if someone sees me" asked Izzy.

"Well if you climb on my hand I'll show you why no one will notice you" replied Penny.

Izzy climbed out and Penny lifted her hand. There on the dashboard was a collection of fairies and elves.

"Oh, are they real" Izzy exclaimed.

"No" laughed Penny "They are pretend but that's why no one will ever know you're there. Everyone is so used to me having fairies and elves about. You didn't notice but there were loads on my window ledge in the office near my desk and I thought I'd find one that looked like you and permanently put it on the dashboard when I'm flying so it won't be noticed if it's you or the pretend one. I'll call it my lucky fairy and say it makes me feel safe."

"Oh, would you do that? Although I don't think it matters. I can do like I did today and ride to the plane in your pocket. I can come out when we're flying and then go in your pocket when we land."

"If you're sure that's how you want it, that's fine. If you change your mind just tell me. I'm sure at home, and maybe even in the office, I'll have something that looks a bit like you. I don't think anyone will really see you unless you fly right past their nose, then they'll not dare say anything in case they are laughed at."

"No, you're probably right. But I'd rather not risk it anyway."

"Coward" laughed Penny.

"I'm not" replied Izzy indignantly.

"I'm only teasing. Now settle down next to 'Miss

12

Pretend' and I'll start the car because we have quite a long drive ahead of us."

"Oh, had I flown a long way then. You said your cottage was not too far from my old home."

"Well actually as you could fly over houses, fields and things you won't have gone as far as we have to in the car. We have to follow roads with the car. If I was in the aeroplane it would be much shorter but I am afraid there is hardly room for the car to stand outside the cottage let alone an aeroplane."

"Oh I see," replied Izzy. "Okay driver, let's hit the road."

Penny started the car and drove out of the car park. Soon they hit the open road. Izzy was spellbound. They travelled through a town where Penny pulled into another car park.

"This is where I do my shopping on the way home from work. I am just popping into this shop to get a few bits of shopping, do you want to come in with me or stay in the car?" asked Penny.

"How can I come in with you?" asked Izzy. "It is during the day and there will be lots of people around."

"Well you can either pop into my bag and have a ride in there or pop into my pocket," suggested Penny.

"Okay then I would love to come with you," replied Izzy. "I think I will ride in your bag. I might be able to peep out occasionally and have a look around as I am curious to see what it looks like inside a shop."

Penny opened her bag and Izzy flew down from her place on the car dashboard. Penny climbed out of the car and picking up her bag and placing it over her shoulder, she locked the car and set off across the car park towards the entrance. Izzy realized that she could peep out of the top of Penny's bag and see where they were going. She found a piece of cotton that she could hang on to so she felt safe and was fascinated by the huge doors as they passed into the store. Penny picked up a basket as they went through the door and proceeded to put various items of shopping into it as they passed through the shop. Izzy just couldn't believe the size of the shop and the vast array of products. Soon Penny had collected all the items she needed and proceeded to the checkout. After paying for the items, Penny headed back to her car. Once inside the car she opened her bag and reached inside and gently lifted Izzy out and placed her back on the dashboard.

"Well Izzy how did you enjoy your first trip to a supermarket?"

"It was fantastic, so huge and so many items on the shelves. How on earth do you know what you need to buy?" asked Izzy.

"Well I just know what I need to cook meals, clean the house, do the washing etc. so I collect the items that I have either run out of or nearly run out of," laughed Penny. "Now shall hit the road again?"

"Yes please," replied Izzy.

After visiting the supermarket they passed some more shops and houses and then headed out into the country. Eventually they drove under a bridge.

"That is where the train that caused you so much aggravation in the past crosses the road," explained Penny.

"I'm glad there isn't one now. I hope I never hear that awful noise again," shuddered Izzy.

"Actually I quite like trains," Penny answered.

"What," shrieked Izzy. "Please say you are joking?"

"Well no, I'm not but they aren't trains like you have encountered," answered Penny.

"What do you mean? What others are there?" queried Izzy.

"The ones I like are steam trains. They are much slower and often travel through beautiful countryside. They make a different sound too."

"How can they? They are just great noisy beasts," replied Izzy.

"One day, when I'm going on one, after I've completed my exams. I'll take you with me. Is that okay? I'll show you what I mean. If you still feel the same you needn't ever go again?"

"Well I'm not sure," replied Izzy, "they shake and rattle you all over."

"A bit, I'll agree, but it is a gentler shake," Penny said.

"Okay, I'm game," agreed Izzy.

"Oh I'm so glad I met you. Life is going to be full of adventures. For example, have you ever seen the sea and sand? Have you ever been on a boat?" asked Penny.

"No. I told you. I'd never been out of the garden before now. Why is the sea near us?"

"Well it is only about 15 or 20 minutes drive away from the cottage but in the opposite direction to your home, sorry old home, so I suppose you won't have visited."

"No, as I said, no one has left the garden for generations."

"Well that is definitely another adventure for our list, we will visit the seaside and I'll see if I can persuade one of the other pilots to go sailing with me as I know Danny can sail."

"But if you go with Danny that means I can't go," wailed Izzy.

"Of course you can. I'll wear something with a pocket in so you can ride in it. Actually, my waterproof jacket has so many pockets you can soon duck into one if Danny turns round. I'm not sure, but he is the only one who doesn't make fun of my collection of little people and I have sometimes caught him lifting them lovingly from the window ledge so he may be a man after my own heart but he is much shyer than me."

"What do you mean? Do you think he believes in fairies and elves? I didn't think any grown up people did?"

"Well I do, as you have found out," answered Penny, "so who says there are not other people, both men and women?"

"I don't know. I suppose you could be right. The problem is, how do you tell?" asked Izzy

"I don't know at the moment, let me sleep on it. By the

way you aren't frightened of little dogs and kittens are you?"

"I don't know. I have never been near any, why?" asked Izzy.

"Well I have a puppy and a kitten at home but I am sure once they get used to you they won't bother you. In fact there is a little door, which they both use, that leads to the garden. It means they can come and go as they please when I am out, which you could probably share with them. That would mean you could go out whenever you wanted to."

"Sounds scary, especially the kitten. Don't they pounce on things that fly?" asked Izzy.

"Well he tries to catch flies and butterflies and things but misses every time."

"Knowing my luck he would catch me," grumbled Izzy. "What about the puppy is he going to be big and growl at me?"

"No she is a little darling, so soft and cuddly and wouldn't catch or hurt a flea."

"Well I reserve judgement. I thought it all sounded too good to be true," Izzy complained.

"Oh don't be a spoilsport," laughed Penny. "We will all get on famously but if you hate it too much you can always join the fairies and elves in the wood."

"Yes I suppose so," replied Izzy, "but I was looking forward to living in your garden, it sounded wonderful."

"Well try it and see how you feel. Don't judge the dog and cat until you meet them."

"No I won't. Are we nearly there yet?" asked Izzy.

"In about 5 minutes we will leave this busy road and turn into the village and then at the other side of the village is a track which is quite bumpy so you will have to hang on. That leads to the cottage. The only people who come down the track are people coming to the cottage, unless they are lost, which sometimes happens."

"Is that all the people we see?" asked Izzy.

"Well sometimes people walk down the track to walk

16

their dogs, people from the village, but they turn off into the wood before they reach the cottage."

"Oh that is okay then, so I could be out in the garden during the day and no one will spot me although I must say I mostly sleep during the day."

"Of course but if you wake early or are not ready for bed when the sun gets up you are safe from prying eyes."

Just then Penny turned off the main road towards the village. When the village came into sight Izzy gasped.

"Is that the village you were talking about? Oh it looks so pretty and sleepy. Why have the houses got funny roofs?"

"What do you mean, funny roofs?" asked Penny.

"Their roofs are sort of straw looking. I don't know, but they don't look like roofs of the houses that I lived near anyway."

"Oh sorry, they have thatched roofs. They are made of straw so I see what you mean. I guess it will look very different to you but I am so used to seeing them I don't notice them now."

"What do you mean, don't notice them, they look strange so you must notice them!" exclaimed Izzy.

"If you look around you will see that nearly all the houses have the same type of roofs and in a lot of ways look the same with little windows and walls around the gardens so I don't notice them. In fact our house looks the same as most of these but we don't live in the actual village but down a lane at the end of the village," answered Penny.

"What" screamed Dizzy, "You mean we live in a little house just like these that I am looking at? Pinch me I must be dreaming this is just the sort of house I have always dreamed of living in!"

Penny laughed, "Honestly, I really live in a tiny cottage which looks just like these that we are passing. Do you see that one, there just on the bend in the road, well that looks just like mine but ours is at the end of a rather long lane next to an enchanted forest, or I tell myself it's enchanted, just so I can indulge in my fantasies. Mind you now I have my very own fairy living with me they may not be fantasies."

"Well I am real enough so why not can't there be other fairies and elves living in the wood next to your house? Have you ever seen any?"

"Actually yes I have, but only fleetingly", laughed Penny, "but now you are going to live with me I might be able to meet them properly."

"Sure if they live in the forest like you say then I will introduce you to them and they might come and use the garden as their home you never know."

"Oh that would be so wonderful if they would," exclaimed Penny, "I would feel so honored if they would visit my garden sometimes but if they set up residence there it would be a dream come true."

"Well I won't promise anything at the moment, let us just wait and see but I will go and see them and put the idea to them and see what they say."

"Oh my goodness that would be great I would be in heaven if that happened. Well this is where we turn off down the lane. Now hold on as it is quite bumpy but that is why no one ever comes down here."

The car turned off the main road and entered a narrow lane. Penny slowed the car down to a crawl but Izzy still had to grab 'Miss Pretend' and hold on to her tightly. Luckily 'Miss Pretend' had a suction base which securely attached her to the dashboard. Suddenly Penny hit an extra large bump and Izzy lost her hold on the pretend fairy and slipped off the dashboard down into the floor underneath Penny's feet. She scrambled as far away as possible to safety as Penny brought the car to a stop.

"Oh Izzy, I'm so sorry," exclaimed Penny. "I forgot I had a real live fairy on the dashboard. I didn't mean to shake you off. Oh where are you? Are you okay? Oh please speak to me!"

Suddenly Izzy emerged and fluttered up and perched on the gear stick.

"My goodness Penny, don't you ever clean under your car seat?" grumbled Izzy. "There are so many rocks under there that poked and prodded me until I will be covered in bruises tomorrow."

"Rocks, what rocks," queried Penny? "I'm sure there are no rocks under the seat. What on earth are you talking about?"

"There are rocks under the seat I'm telling you," exclaimed Izzy.

"Oh it's probably only gravel but I guess it will feel like rocks to you as you are so little," laughed Penny. "So sorry madam I promise next time I hoover out the car I'll make sure I go under the seat. In the meantime where are you going to travel when we are going down the bumpy lane. Obviously it's too bumpy for you to sit on the dashboard but where else would you be safer. Sometimes I wear clothes that have a pocket but not always so that is not a permanent solution but I am struggling to know what to suggest."

Izzy looked about the car.

"Yes, up there, that's the answer," Izzy shouted.

"Where, what are you looking at?" asked Penny.

Izzy unfolded her wings again and fluttered up and landed on the driving mirror.

"Is this okay?" she asked Penny. "Is it okay to sit on here? I can see where we are going but I can use my wings to keep me balanced and hold on to the stem as it's nice and slim."

"Yes that's okay by me if you think you can hang on there," answered Penny. "Maybe I can find something to hang on the mirror that you can sit on. Maybe some soft furry balls or something. Maybe you can always travel there instead of on the dashboard."

"That would be great because it's not too comfortable. Something soft and furry would be ace," mused Izzy.

"Okay then we will go to the car shop at the weekend and see what we can find. In the meantime can you manage on there if I start the car again?" asked Penny.

"Yes of course now I know it is going to be that bumpy I can hang on tighter and keep my wings unfurled to help me to balance. Okay let us have another go. How long is this bumpy lane then?" questioned Izzy.

"Oh just over a mile, 5 or 10 minutes or so and we will be home," answered Penny as she started the car and slowly set off again. Penny tried to miss as many of the bumps as she could and Izzy managed to hang on to the mirror as tightly as she could. They passed fields of corn and even a field of cows.

"Do you think that might be the field of cows where I met Tulip," asked Izzy?

"Maybe, I'm not sure in what direction you came from when you flew into the airfield," answered Penny. "Maybe you can go and visit that field one day and see if you recognize the cows and calves in there."

"Yes I could. Oh wouldn't it be wonderful if I was living this close to Tulip. She was so kind. I'm sure she would be pleased to see me. I could keep her posted on all our adventures then."

"Well if it is the same herd I know the farmer quite well, in fact I buy my eggs from them and sometimes some vegetables, so we can go and visit Tulip even in winter when she has gone into the farm buildings to keep warm."

"Oh I do hope so," exclaimed Izzy, "that would be awesome. Who knows I might be able to ride in Tulip's ear again!"

"You are so easily pleased," laughed Penny. "Let us hope it is then."

"As long as I don't have to encounter the dog from hell though because if that is Tulip's field and you said we weren't that far from my old home and the train track then I might not have flown that far and I might encounter the garden with the dog in it," said Izzy.

"True, unfortunately I can't help you there. You will just have to make sure you don't land in any gardens when you go exploring won't you?"

"Yes I suppose so," answered Izzy. "Are we nearly home yet as my arms are getting tired?"

"Yes just round this bend and you will see the house and driveway. There you are, just in front of us, nestled among the trees."

"Oh my, what a wonderful, pretty little house," exclaimed Izzy. "Are the trees the forest you were telling me about that is at the bottom of the garden?"

"Yes," answered Penny. "That is the forest, we turn into the drive here but you see how the path into the forest is at the other side of the drive. As you can see there is the garage then a hedge before our garden so even people taking their dogs for a walk never see into our back garden. At the bottom of the garden we have a stream with a bridge over it and a gate at the end of the bridge that leads directly into the forest and a little clearing with the waterfall I was telling you about. The actual path into the forest, that people walk their dogs on, swings away from the clearing with lots of trees between so no one ever comes to the clearing but me. I think that is why the elves, pixies and fairies play there because they no one is likely to see them."

"Sounds fabulous. I can't wait to explore it all."

Penny stopped the car and picked up her handbag.

"Right Izzy, shall we start the next adventure and go and see Trixie and Dixie, my puppy and kitten and see what mischief they have got into today. Here jump into my bag and have a ride."

"Great, let's go then Penny and see what the next fun thing is that we are going to do is. I am so glad I landed in your plane this morning to have my sleep. The day just keeps on getting better and better," laughed Izzy as she jumped off the mirror and landed in Penny's bag for her next ride into a whole new world.

Izzy meets Trixie and Dixie

Penny unlocked the front door and went inside. Suddenly a little ball of black fluff came hurtling through an open door and launched itself at Penny. Penny dropped her bag onto the floor and Izzy flew out of the top. Luckily she managed to get her wings to obey her this time and she flew up to the ceiling and perched on the light fitting.

"What on earth is that monster," Izzy shrieked? "It's huge!"

"No Trixie isn't huge," laughed Penny. "She is a tiny puppy not quite fully grown yet. Come on down and say hello, here perch on my finger and let her sniff you, that is how she makes friends. Down Trixie, be gentle, this is Izzy or rather that is Izzy up there on the lightshade. Come on Izzy, don't be afraid she won't hurt you. Look, if it will make you feel better I'll sit on the floor with Trixie on my knee and you can do it in stages. Begin at my shoulder, then edge down my arm until you get on my hand. If you keep your wings unfolded you can fly out of reach anytime you want."

"Oh I'm not sure, I think I feel safer up here," replied Izzy

"Well Trixie lives here too so you will have to meet eventually, better now that I am here to make sure you are safe."

"Okay," Izzy said. "I'll land on your head first I think."

Izzy flew down off the light and lightly landed on Penny's head. She peered down at the wriggling ball of fluff in Penny's lap. Izzy took a deep breath and jumped onto Penny's shoulder. So far so good, the puppy was still squirming in Penny's arms trying to lick her all over. Slowly Izzy edged down Penny's arm, keeping a watchful eye on the dog, until she reached her wrist. Suddenly the dog stopped wriggling and focused on Penny's wrist. Her eyes grew wide and she edged ever so slowly towards Izzy. Izzy was trembling with fright but she stayed where she was. The dog edged closer still, eyes fixed firmly on Izzy. Suddenly Izzy could feel the dog's breath as she breathed in and out but the dog stayed perfectly still. Izzy plucked up all her courage and bent slowly forward until she could just touch the dog's nose. Unfortunately this tickled and the dog sneezed, blowing Izzy off Penny's wrist. Izzy tumbled down onto Penny's leg then righted herself. She looked up at the dog to tell it off for sneezing when she realised the dog looked so surprised at what had just happened. Izzy grew more confident and fluttered up onto Penny's hand again then jumped gracefully onto Dixie's head. There she sat among all the soft cuddly fur and began to laugh.

"Oh this is a lovely warm comfortable seat Penny," she said. "I think I'll just stay here."

"Well that would be one way to get through the flap outside because you won't be strong enough to push it open on your own. Only problem with that is you will have to persuade Trixie to go out, when you want to go out or come in, as the case might be, not just when she wants to go."

"True," laughed Izzy. "I will have to work on that one."

Izzy slid down Trixie's forehead between her eyes and sat on the dog's nose. The dog tried to see her so became all squint eyed. Suddenly the dog shook it's head and Izzy shot off again and landed on the floor in a heap. She righted herself and found herself looking up the dog's nose because Trixie had laid down flat and was just a whisper away from Izzy. Izzy stood up and found she was at eye level with the puppy.

"Now just a minute Trixie you can't keep sneezing and moving fast and tipping me over. We need to come to some arrangement. You need to make slow movements when I am around or else I will spend my time in a heap on the floor and that won't do," demanded Izzy.

The puppy hung its head and looked so sad that Izzy couldn't stay cross long.

"Okay you didn't mean it I can see. Let us be friends

and begin again." With that Izzy jumped up onto the dog's nose and fluttered up to the top of its head and plumped down again. All this time Penny had been holding her breath hoping both would find a way to live together. When Izzy plumped down among the dog's fur Penny laughed.

"Well I see one hurdle has been overcome. I've never known Trixie to keep still so long. Now I wonder where Dixie is she shouldn't be long as she knows it is usually tea time when I come home."

Suddenly there was a 'bong' and Izzy jumped nearly 3 foot or rather 3 inches in the air. Trixie jumped up and began hurtling back down the passage from the room she had come from minutes earlier.

"There we are," said Penny. "Right on cue. Here comes my other little madam."

By this time Izzy had given up trying to hang on to the dog's fur and had taken flight back to Penny. Penny got up from the floor and said,

"Follow me Izzy into the kitchen and we will get these two their tea. If you want to explore the rest of the house please feel free to have a look around."

Penny wandered into the kitchen and Izzy followed her. She reached up into a cupboard and the cutest ball of fluff jumped up on to the working top. Izzy, who had just landed on the same piece of the top, screamed and tried to scramble out of the way. Unfortunately this drew the kitten's attention and she reached out a paw and plonked it on top of Izzy. Everything went dark for Izzy and she shrieked at the top of her voice,

"Penny help it's got me. I can't move, don't let it hurt me!"

Penny scooped up the kitten and released Izzy. Izzy shook out her wings and stretched her back.

"I knew the kitten would catch me," she grumbled. "You said it would be alright but you lied. Now I can't live here."

"Don't be silly Izzy she didn't hurt you," replied

Penny. "Now Dixie behave yourself, this is our very own fairy. Don't hurt her or pounce on her. Here Izzy crawl on to my hand and I'll put Dixie back down and let her sniff you and if she looks as if she is going to hurt you I'll move my hand out of her reach."

Izzy flew on to Penny's other hand away from the kitten and Penny plopped the kitten back onto the working top. Penny slowly lowered her hand on to the top, a safe distance from the kitten. The kitten stretched out a paw, its eyes as wide as saucers. Slowly Penny inched her hand towards the kitten until her hand was touching Dixie's paw.

"Right Izzy, gently touch Dixie's paw and see what she does. It's okay you are quite safe, I'm watching you both very closely."

Tentatively Izzy leaned over and touched the kitten. Oh how soft and silky she was. The kitten stayed completely still, so Izzy became a bit braver and slid down the side of Penny's hand and stood up next to the paw. Still the kitten didn't move a muscle so Izzy became braver still and jumped on to the kitten's paw. The kitten wriggled its fur as it probably tickled her but didn't move from its crouching position. Izzy edged up the paw towards Dixie's nose until she knew she was close enough for Dixie to smell her. Suddenly the kitten rolled over on to her back and dislodged Izzy. Izzy landed on Dixie's chest then as Dixie rolled again she scrambled up her fur on to the side of Dixie's neck.

"Oh look Dixie is playing with you Izzy she isn't trying to catch you at all with her paws and listen she's purring that's her way of saying I love you and I'm happy. I wonder what she will do next?" exclaimed Penny.

Slowly the kitten rolled again, back on to her tummy, and this time Izzy lost her footing and slid down her neck on to the working top between the kitten's paws. The kitten just turned both paws over so Izzy was cupped very gently between her pads and purred even louder.

"Oh you beautiful baby, aren't you sweet," Izzy

murmured. "Are we going to be friends then?"

The kitten just stayed perfectly still as though mesmerised. Izzy gave her a little tap on her nose which made Dixie sneeze blowing poor Izzy across the counter. This seemed to bring Dixie out of her trance and she shook herself, stood up and looked at Penny as much as to say okay, now for some tea please.

Penny clapped her hands.

"There you see nothing to worry about both of my babies have accepted you so you can live with us forever. Now let me get their tea and start a meal for myself. Oh my goodness what are you going to eat? I suddenly realised I have no idea what fairies eat."

"We eat nuts and seeds, maybe a bit of fruit, but remember I am so little I don't eat much at all," answered Izzy.

"No I suppose not. Well I have some seed and nut mixture in the cupboard also seed and fruit mixture as I use it to sprinkle on my yogurt for breakfast."

"Perfect," cried Izzy. "Sounds wonderful but I might try other things now I am living with a human."

"Well please feel free to taste anything you want. I often have things like strawberries, raspberries and blackberries in the fridge but you won't be able to open the door. I will have to find a tiny dish for you to have as your very own fruit bowl and put you some in. I will leave it on the table along with my own fruit bowl that has apples, pears and oranges in but they will be far too big and hard for you. When we go to the supermarket I'll pay more attention to the soft fruit selection and get you different things for you to try. I am not sure what yet but we will investigate together. I also put bird seed out for the birds on their table so you shouldn't starve."

"Doesn't sound like it to me," laughed Izzy. "It all sounds fabulous. Okay Penny you get on with your jobs. I'll just sit here and watch you all. I really think I must be dreaming and I'll suddenly wake up when the train goes rattling by."

"No you aren't dreaming. We are really all here and I have so much to show you. I think we are just going to be fine. I can't wait now for the fun to begin. Looking at everything we do through your eyes, and having to make sure you are safe but included in everything, is going to be a challenge sometimes, but still exciting. Now everyone let's have tea then we will explore the garden before it gets completely dark."

With that Penny put food in the animals' dishes on the floor, refilled their water bowl and raided the cupboard to find a tiny thimble to put some food in for Izzy. All the time she kept up a conversation telling the animals Izzy's story so far and explained things to Izzy as she went along.

Izzy was entranced and didn't want to miss a single thing so although she was quite tired and expected to crawl into a bed straight away she stayed awake and looked forward to exploring the garden with Penny and the animals after tea. She rather hoped that they could venture into the clearing in the forest if there was time if only to see if there was any other fairies out playing tonight although as Izzy had now been awake almost 24 hours she knew she wouldn't be staying with them long, an all-night party would have to wait for another night!

Izzy and the Forest Fairies

After tea was finished and cleared away Penny said,

"Right come on Izzy, I know you are itching to go outside and have a look in the garden. I imagine you are also dying to have a quick peek in the clearing to see if you have other fairies and elves playing there. It is just turning to dusk and a lovely clear, fine night so you might be lucky. Here jump into the pocket of my shirt and have a ride. We will just quickly have a look round the garden so you can get your bearings then cross the bridge and go into the forest. You can explore the garden more on another night in your own time but if I just show you around quickly then you can come back later after I have gone to bed and the animals have settled for the night. If you come back when we aren't there you can meet any animals that visit when all is quiet. Oh hang on a minute I need to feed Hetty, well that is what I call my resident hedgehog, which I have seen out and about in the garden about now. I think she lives, well I say she, but I really don't know if it is male or female, under the summer house. I usually put her food and milk out just under the decking where Dixie and Trixie can't reach it but she can."

"You mean you know you have a hedgehog living here already," queried Izzy. "Do you know of any other animals?"

"Well I would imagine there are mice about too maybe even more than one hedgehog but I've only ever seen one at a time so I don't know. That can be your job Izzy, to find out exactly who is living in my garden and if I can help them live there more happily by planting different flowers and plants or even ensuring I put the right sort of food down. You might even persuade some of the young fairies and elves to settle in my garden. We might be able to make proper little residences for them making some warm and cosy houses to stay in. I've often wondered if they stay in the forest in winter when it's cold and wet and not much food about!"

"Well, at home, we stayed where we were but tried to find warm and dry corners to tuck into in the garden shed, summer house and nooks and crannies in the house walls. No one came out into the garden in winter and even the gardener didn't do too much after he had tidied up the fallen leaves and took the dead heads off the flowers at the end of autumn. We didn't tend to venture outside much in winter as we had usually stored away enough food to last us through the winter. We would have loved more original homes, or I would anyway, like special little fairy houses or old pots, pans or kettles, anything like that. Maybe we can spend the autumn building some villages of old pots and pans in sheltered parts of the garden and lining them with fur, feathers, dandelion clocks, you know the soft downy seeds that blow about, ready for the winter. If there are rabbits in the forest, and I'm sure there will be, maybe they will donate us some fur or better still persuade them to take up residence close to the garden and come and play with us fairies. I would imagine forest fairies might share the squirrels' winter homes as the animals would keep them company. Have we any suitable trees that we could build homes for squirrels do you think as they are messy eaters and leave lots of left-overs after their meals for us fairies. I'm sure with your strength and my knowledge we can actually make your garden a magical fairy garden and even in winter you can watch us through your windows when it's too cold for you to sit around outside. Fairies always have both a summer and winter ball and sometimes even a spring and autumn ball where all the fairies get together from miles around to sing, dance, eat and generally have lots of fun. I've never actually been to one as my family never left the garden and our garden was just not magical enough for a fairy ball. It takes ages to get it ready as we need lots of tables, chairs and a fairy ring marked out to dance in. Toadstools make excellent stages for the bands and performers to use. We need lots of drinking containers as we get very thirsty, especially at the summer ball, that we can dip our cups in. Special pebbles and stones make good water containers for the dewdrops to gather in especially if we build a tiny platform to get them slightly off the ground. Pieces of bark or large leaves will do for this. We also like lots of bushes and flowers with soft petals that we can crawl under or into, especially if they smell nice too, to sleep in when we are tired as usually the ball lasts a few nights. If we are lucky we might get our fairy queen to come for an evening but we will have to build an extra special place for that to happen. I would love to organise one as it has always been my dream but I have never had a proper garden to do it in before. As soon as a leaf fell off a plant or a bit of bark ended up in the garden the gardener quickly picked it up. As for toadstools no way were they allowed to survive or any pebble that wasn't in its correct place allowed to stay there. I used to sometimes think the gardener actually measured the exact spot where things were supposed to be."

"Well I can assure you my garden is definitely not measured," laughed Penny. "I try to sweep up the majority of the leaves in autumn from the trees and hedges in the garden but several escape the sweeping brush! As for pebbles and stones they just seem to appear overnight and they are haphazardly strewn about under shrubs and things. I try not to have too many on the lawn as otherwise I would break the lawnmower but I am happy to work alongside your ideas and suggestions to make it a magical place. Are you serious, do you think between us we could build a garden fit for a fairy ball? That would be fantastic. You can count on me to help in any way I can."

"By the sounds of it you could already have the basics in place and if pebbles and stones appear you could maybe already have a few fairies using your garden. If so all we have to do is spread the word that a friendly human lives here and any big job that needs doing you will only need to be asked and we will do the rest. You can keep a look out or we can do it together to build some suitable winter residences as we have plenty of time over the summer to do that. The fairies from the forest will bring some toadstool spores to plant for the stages as we normally have lots of different areas with different music going every night. I heard from a visiting fairy to our garden that the biggest balls can last as long as 7-10 nights but generally it is more like 3-5 nights. Anyhow that's for the future in the meantime let us go and explore this garden a bit then head out to the clearing. I don't think I'll be staying long tonight as it has been a long, but so exciting day today, and I'm ready for bed but maybe I'll sleep all day tomorrow so I can join the rest of the fairies for a longer party tomorrow night."

By this time Penny, with Izzy in her pocket, had left the house through the back door stepping onto a small patio. Penny paused to breathe deeply at the air and the perfumes from her flowers before stepping off the patio on to a small grassed area. It was good to tell the puppy played here as there was a couple of balls, a dog toy, an old bone and a few chewed up feathers strewn about but round the edges of the lawn was a profusion of beautiful coloured flowers haphazardly growing together. As far as Izzy could see there was no pattern to it all but she could hear the buzzing of the bees collecting their final load of pollen before settling for the night. She imagined that during the day this garden would be alive with bees and butterflies going about their daily lives. She could just hear the gurgling of the stream festooned with rushes along its banks. Oh this was the perfect place to hold a ball. The stream offered an alternative mode of transport for those who wanted to use it and would provide lots of dragonflies to go for a ride on. Usually the fairy queen arrived at a ball by sailing in so this would be perfect. There was a variation of trees of all sizes providing shelter and shade with branches intertwining with the flowers. A dear little summerhouse nestled in a corner of the garden with a rocking chair on its veranda. There were roses climbing up its walls at the side and a pinnacle roof with an old weather vane in the shape of a cockerel perched on top. Izzy guessed the hedgehog family, she was sure there would be more than one in this wildlife haven, lived under the summerhouse and the veranda offered a perfect sanctuary to come out from to feed. Izzy clapped her hands in delight.

"Oh Penny this is the most perfect garden I could ever have imagined. How have you developed it in such a perfect way? You have made a fairy paradise here."

"Well to be honest I didn't actually plan it. It was very overgrown and neglected when I moved in, full of nettles, thistles and other weeds. All I did was slowly bit by bit clear the weeds and built the summerhouse in the corner and the rest sort of grew up on its own. I guess the flowers were already there but couldn't grow because the weeds were stifling them but once I cleared the weeds they could flourish. I must admit some of the smaller trees have grown since I moved in so I guess the birds may have been responsible for them. I have always loved roses, especially climbing fragrant ones, so I bought that plant and planted it next to the summerhouse and it has just taken off, climbing all over the house and veranda. It smells heavenly on a summer evening and I often bring my coffee and sometimes my evening meal out here on a warm summer evening. I take it from your reaction I, or rather the birds and the bees, haven't done too bad a job then?" laughed Penny.

"You have done a fantastic job," answered Izzy, "and looking at the layout I am sure if you haven't fairies living here, they frequently visit. See here you have a tiny fairy ring of white pebbles. It isn't very big suggesting to me that there is only a few using it or maybe they are testing you out to see if you noticed and moved the stones away."

By this time Izzy had fluttered down to the ground to point out the tiny ring.

"And see here a few tiny seeds around a table."

"Oh my goodness so there is I just hadn't noticed them, not even the ring, it just looks so natural there," exclaimed Penny.

"That's how we build our fairy gardens," explained Izzy. "We place things around so everything looks natural. That way the humans don't notice the changes. Here, look we have another table and chairs at the edge of this plant. The plant will provide shelter if it rains."

Penny wandered after Izzy who was fluttering about excitedly showing Penny the tiny signs of fairy existence and animal and insect activity until they arrived at the stream near the bridge.

"Oh look Penny you already have four tiny boats moored off this jetty. The fairies must use them to cross to the other side of the stream when they are preparing to bring things into your garden from the forest," shrieked Izzy. "That means they are busy extending their kingdom into your garden. They must have already decided this was the perfect place for a new kingdom."

"Where are the boats? I don't see any only four tiny twigs caught in the weeds."

"No look closely those twigs are tied with a strand of cotton to this large piece of bark jutting out from the rushes. That is clearly the jetty but these boats are not being used tonight. There may be others on the other side though."

Penny crouched down to take a closer look at what Izzy was pointing to and realised that Izzy was right and a tiny thread was tied to the piece of bark.

"Oh the little darlings. I can see what you mean now but I wouldn't have noticed it without you pointing it out."

Izzy flew over the stream to the other side.

"Yes," she shrieked. "Come and look Penny there are a lot of boats moored at this side a bit bigger than the ones left behind. That means they are intending to bring things back to your garden tonight possibly some more tables and chairs as they will require the bigger boats. Oh hurry up and let us go into the forest and see what they are busy with."

"Just let me put Hetty's food and milk down under the summerhouse veranda and then I'll be with you," answered Penny.

"Well, be quick then, oh okay I'll come with you to see if I can see any hedgehog tracks while you do that. There may be more than one. Yes there is definitely more than one, there are tracks coming from here, and here, oh how sweet. Penny just under here, quite near the front of the veranda, is a hedgehog nest with babies in. Hello Mrs Hedgehog, I'm Izzy and I've come to live with Penny who puts your food out for you. It is okay you can come out when she is there she won't hurt you. How many more of you live here?"

"Well, I was the first one to find this wonderful garden but then a couple more pairs joined me. I quickly realised, Penny as you called her, wouldn't hurt me and seemed pleased when she caught a glimpse of me as I was feeding but I usually wait until she has put the food out and gone back inside before I venture out especially now that I have babies to care for. One of the other hedgehogs has just finished making her nest and was telling me the other day that she didn't think it would be long before her babies were born. My mate unfortunately got run over so I am on my own but I have noticed another male has started to come into the garden from the forest so he might take up residence here."

Izzy emerged from under the summerhouse,

"Hey Penny, you will have to find some more names for your hedgehogs. You have Hetty who has a brood of five babies all with their eyes open so they won't be long before they venture out into the garden and then another two pairs, one that is about to give birth, and a lone male who is only visiting at the moment but that Hetty hopes will take up residence here. I think she rather hopes he will pair up with her as her other mate got run over."

"Oh Izzy, how wonderful. I'll sort out some more bowls to put food and milk out for them all. Thank you for telling me and yes I will try and think up some names for them all. Do you think they might one day trust me enough to come out when I am here working in the garden or when I'm sitting in the chair outside the summerhouse?"

"I should imagine so. Oh look here comes Hetty right on cue and yes look over there another couple emerging and yes here comes the last couple. Oh look that must be the lone male there coming over the bridge," laughed Izzy. "There you are Penny, you see you have lots of hedgehogs. Now get that food put out and tomorrow night you had better bring out some extra and we will get going. Don't worry I think you will be seeing these families many times from now on. Thanks Hetty and the rest of you for being brave enough to come out and show Penny you are all here."

"No thank you Izzy, for letting us know we are safe here and thank you Penny, for creating such a wonderful garden," answered Hetty

"Oh my goodness not only have I my own fairy that I can talk to but I can actually talk to the animals in my garden. It truly is a magic garden," breathed Penny. "Okay Izzy lets go. Bye my special friends enjoy your supper."

Penny straightened up and walked over the bridge to the other side. Yes she could see what had excited Izzy so much. There must have been nearly twenty twigs anchored along the side of the stream. Some didn't appear to be anything more than caught in the reeds and rushes but she guessed the moorings were too tiny for her to see.

"Yes I can see them Izzy," laughed Penny. "Okay let us go through the gate, oh sorry silly me you can fly over it, but let me get through it and I'll follow you. Remember I need to stick to the path I can't fly like you."

Izzy flew ahead of Penny following the path until suddenly the path opened on to the most beautiful tiny clearing that Izzy had ever seen. There was a waterfall flowing into a pool which drained away to the side disappearing once again into the forest.

"Oh it's so beautiful," breathed Izzy. "Absolutely enchanting. Come on Penny sit down and keep still and I will try and encourage all these fairies to come out of hiding and carry on with their fun. They are probably having a break and a swim before continuing with their nights work. They will be waiting until you go to bed before arriving back into your garden with their allocated items."

Izzy jumped on to a protruding rock at the side of the pool and called,

"Okay all you fairies, elves and pixies you can come out of hiding. I know you are there as I can see some of you behind stones and grass. Penny here is my best friend and she can see us fairies so she will not harm us. It is her garden you are working on and she will help you all she can if we need a human strength to move anything. I have already met her puppy and kitten and neither have harmed me so we should be able to all use the garden at all times and be safe."

Slowly bit by bit fairies and elves emerged from their hiding places until the clearing was buzzing with voices and movement. Izzy leapt down from her rock and flew over to Penny.

"See here I am on Penny's finger. I'm Izzy and I left home to seek my own new perfect garden and join a new kingdom. I accidently met up with Penny and she brought me home with her. Now anyone who wants to come and say hello feel free and ask her or me anything you want to know."

Suddenly Penny was covered in fairies and elves all trying to talk at once. She could feel them in her hair, perched on her ears, fingers, hands, arms and even one was sat on her nose. That one tickled and she hoped she wouldn't sneeze and blow her off! Poor Penny couldn't make head nor tail of all the chatter so she just sat perfectly still in complete awe of both Izzy and how her life had changed in a mere few hours.

Suddenly Izzy clapped her hands and the chatter ceased.

"It's no good you all talking at once we can't answer you all at the same time. Now if you want to say a personal hello or ask a question, form an orderly queue and one by one fly on to Penny's hand, tell us your name and ask your question. Penny, I suggest you lay your hand on your knee, as this may take some time as I didn't realise you had quite so many fairies living in the area of your garden and I think your hand might get tired. Right one at a time please."

A beautiful tiny fairy wearing a pink and silver dress flew down directly on to Penny's hand and gave a little curtsey. "I am Mercury. At the moment my sister, Topaz, and me seem to be head of this kingdom. We also left home a while ago as we lost our home when they cleared our meadow to build houses on and we accidently found this clearing. Bit by bit others have joined us for various reasons and we have just got larger and larger. We welcome you Izzy as you seem to be a born leader and hope you will be happy with us. Topaz and I haven't enough experience to lead a kingdom this big and I hope you might give us the honour of becoming our fairy queen. Me, Topaz, Sapphire and Emerald will be all happy to serve you as our queen as second in command. We knew whoever it was that lived in the house was happy to keep the garden wild and untamed and made the decision after last winter to try to make it into our new kingdom headquarters. We found there was really not enough shelter for us all here so began in the spring to venture out from the clearing to find something better. We spied the garden and watched from the trees to see who lived there and if we felt it could be transformed without the owner noticing. Penny, you proved more than good enough to let us continue our work and so we have begun to extend it. You never dislodged our boats, scattered our ring or discarded our tables and chairs so we are now stepping up the work so we have it ready to hold our own fairy ball next month. We have a lot of work to get through and I don't imagine it will be good enough to invite the chief fairy queen to attend this one but maybe with your help we can get it ready to receive the queen for a later one. Here Topaz, Sapphire and Emerald come and say hello to Izzy, who if she accepts will become our new queen, and Penny, who I am sure will be a great help to us. Obviously it is most important to bring the garden on during the summer and autumn ready for us all to have places to live, keep warm and store food for the winter as well as prepare for the balls. Now we have a resident queen we will have to step up our standards to ensure she is not embarrassed when other kingdom heads come to stay."

"Hi Mercury, Topaz, Sapphire and Emerald it is great to meet you and I will be very honoured to become your queen but I will be a hands on queen helping to plan, and work if necessary, to make Penny's garden the best kingdom that there has ever been. As my subjects I hope I can make you happy and ensure, along with Penny and all her animals that already reside in the garden, that we can provide enough food, shelter and homes for you all and your families. Let us make a pact to all work, live and play together and include Penny in all our activities whenever possible. Mercury were you planning on just the summer and winter balls or were you thinking about an autumn one too?"

"Well," said Mercury, "of course it would be lovely to be able to have all four fairy balls Spring, Summer, Autumn and Winter balls but we felt that it might be too much work to get ready for three balls and set up the kingdom ready for winter but if we have lots of help from Penny then it might be possible to get it all ready. The summer one will have to be a very small one just to reward everyone for all their hard work up to press. Maybe if we get on well with the building of winter residences and things we can reward them with another in Autumn as you know all fairies, elves and pixies love to party but it will depend on how all the work progresses."

"Sounds an excellent plan Mercury," answered Izzy already taking charge. "A small intimate one next month just this kingdom, a larger one in autumn then we go for a big national one for winter. Does anyone know where the national one held? Is it still the summer one or winter? The

38

garden I lived in before never held even small balls nor did we attend any but I remember a year or two ago a passing fairy said they were travelling to the Summer National Ball and just briefly stopped for a rest. They didn't stay long because they didn't like our garden and quickly flew off. Since then I have always wanted to attend one but never thought I would have my own kingdom to host one."

"Oh it is still the Summer National Ball usually held in Cornwall at the very bottom tip of England. We have never been but have often had passing fairies stop on route. I don't think anyone has ever thought about holding a full Winter Ball, most kingdoms have a small one but never a big national one. I think everyone has shied away from it as it is very cold at that time of year and often a shortage of food and things. I mean, where could we hold it if the weather is very bad and we have lots of guests?" asked Mercury

"Well in Penny's summerhouse of course," answered Izzy. "We will be warm and dry and I'm sure between Penny and me we can conjure up enough food for masses of guests. Think of the fun we could have. We could organise different games, different music and food than is normally served. Get ourselves known as the alternative ball."

"Wow that sounds exciting. What do you think Penny, are you game for us to use your summerhouse to hold a National Winter Fairy Ball in?" Mercury queried.

Penny finally found her voice.

"Of course you can, I'll be honoured. Please feel free to do anything you want and tell me if I can do anything to help. So sorry, Mercury, Topaz, Sapphire and Emerald I am forgetting my manners, I am pleased to meet you. I am speechless I hoped one day I would be able to have a fairy garden and that some might use it to play in but this, hosting the Winter National Fairy Ball, is beyond my wildest dreams. And to top it off my own little fairy, Izzy, has been crowned queen of this kingdom. Oh does this mean you won't live with me, Trixie and Dixie anymore or come on any adventures with me?" exclaimed Penny.

Izzy laughed.

"No I will be honoured and pleased to continue to live with you in the house Penny, and actually going on adventures with you will be beneficial to my kingdom as I will be able to meet fairies, pixies and elves from a lot further afield than if I just stay here. We can become the national headquarters maybe one day or even, if we travel to other countries together, international headquarters. Who knows what the future holds?"

"Okay Penny and Izzy thank you. Now we will make room for the rest of the kingdom to come and pay tribute to their new Queen and her human friend." Mercury curtseyed and turned to the other fairies all waiting patiently in line.

"Izzy has been elected as our new queen and she will receive you all now. Come up and say hello and tell her your name and any gifts or talents that you bring to her kingdom," instructed Mercury.

With another curtsey to Izzy and Penny she took her place at the side of Izzy with Topaz curtseying going to the other side. Sapphire and Emerald followed suit so that Izzy was flanked on each side by two fairies to show they were next in command then each fairy, elf and pixie took their turn to fly onto Penny's hand and introduce themselves. Penny knew she would never remember all the names and eventually Izzy also laughed.

"I'll never remember you all so I'm saying sorry now. Hopefully as we all work together I'll get you all sorted out in my memory but anyway it was lovely to meet you all. What are your plans for the rest of the night?"

"Well now we know Penny is okay we can load up the boats with some different seeds, tables and chairs as well as several more white pebbles for the fairy ring in the garden. Is there any particular spot where you do or don't want the fairy ring to be Penny?" answered Mercury.

"Well not really but it will be best if it isn't on the grass as I have to mow it every few days in summer and it will mean it gets disturbed but anywhere else is fine by me."

"Great Penny, we had already started it off just to the side of the steps leading up to the summerhouse veranda as that is the ideal place. The rose will provide lots of sleeping accommodation in the flowers, it won't get trodden on if people go into the summerhouse as we want you to be able to still use the summer house and it will in fact be ideal for you to sit in your chair and watch us when we have a party. There is plenty of space all around it to place tables and chairs and if we need to put extensions on to the tables for the ball we can and at the other side of the steps tucked around the corner we can plant the toadstools for the bands and performers so they can be seen by the guests but not right on top of them. It is okay don't panic we won't allow any toadstools to grow that will harm Dixie or Trixie although as yet we haven't encountered her much. Dixie often comes and watches us at work just before we finish for the night although she can be a minx as sometimes she deliberately moves a stone we have carefully placed or digs up a seed we have planted."

Penny laughed

"That sounds about right for her! I did wonder where she went early in the morning as she often strolls in, just as I am getting up for work, full of her own importance. I guess that was why she didn't hurt you Izzy, she was used to seeing fairies in the garden but having one in the house kind of threw her a bit at first."

"Yes, I guess so," answered Izzy laughing, "and maybe Trixie also knows about fairies too. You see Penny, although you didn't know it, you had already started the ball rolling to get your own fairy kingdom at the bottom of your garden."

"Well it is such a perfect place we, the fairies, are proud to live there. Are you joining us for the night Izzy?" asked Mercury.

"To be honest, Mercury, I think I'll call it a day. I haven't been to bed since early evening yesterday but I'll be out to join you tomorrow night and we can plan how we are going to improve Penny's garden and make it into an enchanted magical place for the Winter National Ball. We can then also work out how Penny can help too."

"Yes I'm going back into the house too," answered Penny, "but thank you all so much for being brave enough to come out and meet me and for using my garden as your new kingdom headquarters. I will help all I can. What about some large logs which will provide homes for insects and beetles and I'll certainly go and look in junk shops for old pans and kettles to place around the garden. During the summer Izzy and I can collect bits of sheep wool from fences and places to line them with which will make them cosy and warm for winter. In fact I will have a look in the attic as I brought some old pots and pans from my granny's house when I cleared it out. I remember thinking they would make some unusual homes for animals and birds to nest in or I could use them as planters."

"Sounds like you already have some good ideas. Yes logs are good, as it helps provide homes for beetles and insects like you said. Are you aware you have some hedgehogs living under the summerhouse and some mice as well living in the garden? You have a family of water voles busy making homes along the banks of the stream behind the summerhouse. We tend to use beetles and ants to help us move some of the bigger pieces of vegetation so providing them with homes, saves us having to persuade them to come into the garden from the forest. Right I'll leave you and get these boats loaded. See you tomorrow Izzy and you Penny whenever you want. I think we will make you an honorary queen Penny," suggested Mercury "if that is okay by you."

"Oh I don't think I can aspire to be a queen," laughed Penny, "even an honorary one of a Fairy Kingdom. It is far too grand for me. Do Fairy Kingdoms have names at all, because if they do you will have to get your heads together and think of a name for it."

"Penny's Kingdom," chorused Izzy, Mercury, Topaz,

Sapphire and Emerald all together. "We will call our kingdom 'Penny's Kingdom' in honour of all the work you started and the fact that you have allowed us free access to your garden and summerhouse."

"Oh my goodness things just get better and better and if any of you or your subjects need to come into the house for any reason please feel free to do so."

"I don't think we will need the house but the overhang from the patio might prove useful at some point," replied Mercury.

"Fine, feel free to use whatever bit of the garden you need. I promise I won't move anything without asking one of you first," promised Penny. "Now all of you, I'm going indoors as I think it will be bedtime soon and I need to do some more coursework before tomorrow, as I still have several pieces to finish before my final exams in three weeks."

"That's perfect," Mercury said, "as the Summer Ball is just four weeks away. That means you can spend the evening watching the party and listening to the music as a treat after all your hard work. What exams are you taking?"

Before Penny could reply Izzy had answered for her.

"Penny flies one of those great big metal birds that we see in the sky. The ones that make a lot of noise and she took me with her today and what is more she has promised me I can go with her any day I want. We are also going on lots of adventures like to the seaside and other places so I will be able to advertise our National Winter Fairy Ball. I am sure there must be lots of different fairy kingdoms and wouldn't it be great to meet them?"

"Wow sounds fantastic," Topaz exclaimed, "like you Izzy I'm sure there are other different fairy kingdoms from ours. Think of all the ideas we could swap if we could meet them. I am so glad Mercury elected you our new queen Izzy, and yes Penny, you will play an equally important role helping to make our kingdom the best in the world. Lovely to meet you both and we will see you another night."

"Goodnight," Mercury, Sapphire and Emerald chorused.

"Goodnight," replied Izzy and Penny as they left the clearing.

"What an exciting night, well I suppose exciting day all round wouldn't you say Izzy?" asked Penny.

"Definitely," agreed Izzy.

"Next question we need to think about Izzy, is where are you going to sleep? What can I provide to satisfy a newly elected Fairy Queen your majesty?" laughed Penny.

"Well you have also become a queen too Penny so how is it going to change the place you sleep?"

"Point taken Izzy I guess I'll just treat you the same as I have all day. But seriously, where are you going to sleep?"

"Well to be honest Penny I am so tired I could curl up anywhere but let us go in and explore the rest of your house maybe something will just jump out at us."

"Okay, oh I know I have a lovely little wooden trinket box on my bedroom windowsill. I don't actually remember what is in it but I know I never use it for anything important and I have some cotton wool balls in the bathroom so we can probably use them to line it. It should make a cosy bed for you and as I always have my bedroom window slightly open you can come and go as you please both day and night. I leave the bedroom door open when I go to bed as Trixie always sleeps on the bed with me. Dixie usually starts the night on the bed but isn't usually still there when I get up. After tonight I now know why and what she gets up to. I don't allow the animals to go into the bedroom when I'm not there so you can have an undisturbed sleep during the day."

"Wow that sounds brilliant Penny," Izzy replied. "Can we sort my bed out now before you start your coursework as I really am very tired?"

"Yes I suppose you will be because you travelled all night and had just got to sleep when I climbed into the aeroplane."

"True," laughed Izzy, "but I wouldn't have changed a minute of today. I think you must be lucky for me as I haven't had so much fun and excitement in all my life, as I have today. If the rest of our life together is so good then I'll burst with excitement."

"Oh please don't do that Izzy because if you burst you won't be able to fulfil your duties as the Queen of Penny's Kingdom. After all you now have responsibilities to your subjects. You have promised them an Autumn and National Winter Fairy Ball so you will have to deliver."

"Okay," laughed Izzy, "but please let us go and make my bed as I haven't even the energy to fly up the stairs."

"Well in that case my beautiful fairy queen hop in my shirt pocket and you can have a ride."

Penny found that the trinket box was actually empty so she quickly made up a base of cotton wool that she found in the bathroom cupboard and placed lots of cotton wool balls on top so Izzy could bury herself in them. Izzy snuggled down immediately and with a sleepy goodnight fell asleep. Penny went back downstairs and got her books out and settled down to some serious study before heading to bed. She had a quick peek in the box before she settled herself and the animals for the night and sure enough Izzy was still fast asleep. I wonder what tomorrow will bring thought Penny before she drifted off to sleep herself.

A New Day

Penny awoke, as usual, when her alarm went off the next morning. She lay still for a few moments thinking about the beautiful dream she had been having about finding a dear little fairy in her aeroplane who had come home with her and the fairy had been made the Fairy Queen of the area. Suddenly Penny became aware of a tickling sensation on her hand.

"Dixie stop tickling my hand with your whiskers you silly cat. Give me a minute and I will get up," Penny said.

"It is not Dixie it is me," laughed Izzy. "Don't you remember that I joined you for the day yesterday? Thank you for my wonderful bed it was so cosy and warm that I never woke up once."

Penny opened her eyes and saw the tiny fairy of her dream sat on her hand. Trixie was laid on one side of Penny watching the fairy but making no attempt to catch her and Dixie was on the other side.

"Oh you are real I thought I had dreamt about you. I still cannot believe you came home with me! Did it really happen that we met the fairies and elves from the forest and they made you their Fairy Queen?"

"Yes it was certainly no dream. Look Dixie and Trixie have accepted me too. Trixie and I have been playing until that horrible noise went off then Trixie returned to sit on the bed so I came and landed on your hand. Dixie was watching us too and as you can see neither of them have tried to hurt me."

Penny sat up completely awake now.

"Oh Izzy that is fantastic. It means you are safe here and can come and go as you please. I will leave the bedroom window open a tiny bit so you can come and rest in your bed whenever you want but I will also have a look around the backdoor as I think there may be a tiny hole just at the bottom. If it is too small for you I can make it a bit bigger. I thought about it last night but it is near the pet flap and I was worried that Dixie and Trixie might try to catch you if you used that as your door. You will not be strong enough to push the pet door open unless you hitch a lift with one of the animals."

"It is okay Penny I found the tiny hole this morning when I was exploring. I could feel the wind when I was looking at the pet flap after Dixie had gone out into the garden so I went to examine it. It is a tight squeeze but I managed it this morning. If you could just make it a tiny bit bigger that would be great although it will that mean you get a bigger draft?"

"Well I suppose it would but hang on a minute, why don't I actually make you your very own door somewhere? One that has a handle on so you can come and go as you please but we don't get a draft into the house. It is not so bad in summer but in winter we try to block up as many draft holes as we can to keep the house cosy and warm. Give me chance to give it some thought but in the meantime I will make the hole a bit bigger for you when I come downstairs as a temporary door for the next few days and then try and design you your very own door so you can go outside or come in at the same time as Trixie and Dixie. It will allow you to play with the animals if you want during the day whilst I am at work otherwise the only way you can get into the house will be my bedroom window and as I shut the door during the day you won't be able to join Trixie and Dixie in any games in the house just in the garden."

"Oh that sounds like a wonderful idea my very own door. Can I help you to design it?" asked Izzy.

"Of course you can help to design it," laughed Penny, "provided you don't make it a too complicated shape. I have quite good woodworking skills but wouldn't be able to do anything too ambitious. What sort of shape is your favourite shape round or square?"

"Oh definitely round, would that be possible?" answered Izzy. "I would love a round door if that would be possible."

"Well," answered Penny, " a round door is probably the easiest as I can easily make a round hole in the wooden door next to the animal's door but give me the chance to have a proper think about it and we will discuss it tonight when I get back from work. Now I must get up and have a shower and get dressed. Please move you two, or I suppose I should say three, although you are so light Izzy I can't feel you except as a tickling sensation on my skin. Come on move Trixie, time to get up, and I don't want to hear that either of you animals have got up to mischief while I have been at work, as I now have Izzy to tell me all about your antics during the day. You won't be able to keep secrets from me anymore," laughed Penny as she climbed out of bed.

"Don't worry Trixie and Dixie I won't tell Penny about any mischief. Your secrets will be safe with me. In fact most of the time I will probably be helping you to get into mischief," answered Izzy.

"A fine Fairy Queen you are going to make if you are going to encourage and aid my pets in getting up to mischief. What are your subjects going to think if they see you misbehaving?" laughed Penny.

"Well like I told them last night, I will be a hands on queen and as you know fairies and elves love to party, dance and generally have fun and yes, providing no one gets hurt, they get up to mischief, so I imagine they will admire their queen if she shows she can share their fun. Anyhow if it doesn't work like that then we have a problem as I don't intend to become serious and boring. After all that was the reason I left home because life was so boring. Now I have found my perfect life I intend to live it to the full and have a great time leading my kingdom. Just as I would want leading if I was an ordinary subject. I would admire my queen much more if she got off her throne and joined in whatever we were doing, I can assure you," exclaimed Izzy.

"Okay," laughed Penny, "please don't go all defensive on me I was just joking. As I don't know how Fairy

Queens behave normally as I have never met one before, then who am I to advise you how to behave. Now I am going for a shower and get myself dressed because if I don't get a move on I won't have time to enlarge the hole for you Izzy, have any breakfast myself or feed you all."

Penny turned on the shower to warm up while she cleaned her teeth with Izzy sitting perched on the tap watching what she was doing. While Penny had a shower, Izzy sat on the shower curtain rail as she had found that the shower head was too warm to sit on and if she sat on the tap she got sprayed with water, so the curtain rail was the best option. Penny quickly dressed and Izzy, Dixie and Trixie followed her downstairs. Penny filled the kettle and turned it on to boil. She popped some biscuits in the animal's bowls and popped some seed and fruit mix in Izzy's thimble that she had used last night. By this time the kettle had boiled so Penny made herself a cup of coffee, put some cereal in a bowl and popped a couple of slices of bread in the toaster. She poured herself some juice and carried her breakfast over to the table.

"I will enlarge your hole after my breakfast," she informed Izzy. "I can do it while my tea cools down a bit. I will visit the supermarket when I leave work tonight to try and find you some soft fruit to make up your own fruit bowl, so you have something to snack on during the day. I am not actually sure what I am looking for but I am sure something will inspire me when I get there. Are you staying here today Izzy or coming to work with me?"

"No I think I will stay here today as there is a lot more of the garden to explore yet that I haven't seen. I will make a note of all the places that might be nice and sheltered to place some containers in for our subjects to live in during the winter. Did you say you thought you had some old pans and things in the attic?" asked Izzy.

"Yes I put a lot up in the attic when I cleared out my Grandma's cottage. I intended to put them in the garden as unusual planters or as nesting sites for the birds in the garden. I expected to be planting flowers or making homes for birds though, not fairies and elves," laughed Penny.

"Well unknown to you there might have been fairies and elves living among the plants if you had used them but this way we can make them lovely and cosy for winter homes now you know who is waiting to make your garden their fairy town. Did your Grandma believe in fairies too Penny?" asked Izzy.

"Yes it was through her that my love of fairies began. My parents travelled a lot for work, as both were in the military, so when they were away I stayed with my grandmother. They were killed in a car crash when I was a young teenager so I went to live permanently with my Grandma and she used to encourage me to go and talk to the fairies when I was feeling lonely down at the bottom of the garden. Sometimes we went together and sat on a tree stump and my Grandma used to teach me to listen to the sounds in the garden like the popping of the gorse, the rustling of the leaves or the wind whistling through the trees. She used to tell me stories about fairies and elves. The popping of the gorse was the fairies and elves having a big celebration with fireworks and the rustling of the leaves was them using the leaves as trampolines. She could describe their antics so well that I am now sure she, like me, had the gift to enter their world and not only see them but also communicate with them. In fact her cottage was very like this one that I live in. Her garden was not a big garden but always a riot of colour with many beautiful flowers but nothing fancy. She had bluebells, snowdrops, daffodils, cornflowers, sweet peas and a host of other flowers. The lawn, if you could call it that, had speedwell and dandelions growing in it and tiny yellow flowers amongst the green. She used to say the speedwell was used by the fairies as tea because it was a healing plant, and the fairies needed the dandelion seeds to ride on to attend the balls as they were often a long journey away. Whenever she saw the dandelion seeds blowing in the wind she used to say it was the fairies and elves going off on a very long journey possibly over the sea to far off lands. I guess, slowly, I absorbed all her stories and in the early days after my parents were killed I found solace at the bottom of the garden among the fairies. I never felt it mattered if the fairies and elves saw me crying or even just being sad, whereas I tried to hide that sadness from my Grandma, as she had also lost her only daughter, and my school friends as I didn't want their pity. On reflection I think my Grandma also found solace amongst her fairies as I often found her at the bottom of the garden when I came home from school. I knew that I could not live in my Grandma's house after she died as my ambition to be a pilot meant that I needed to be close to a training school. Like my parents I had tried the military, where I got my taste for flying, but quickly realised that the harsh military lifestyle was not for me but that I wanted to train to be an airline pilot. I have nearly finished my training and would love to combine my skill as a pilot with helping other people, possibly in a medical field. I had wanted to be a doctor or something medical, which is why I had joined the military, but I never completed my training as I was too homesick. Once I am trained as a pilot I will look around for an opening to combine helping people with flying I think," answered Penny.

"Does that mean you will be moving away from this dear little cottage?" wailed Izzy. "Just when I have found my perfect garden and become the Fairy Queen too! Oh please tell me you don't mean it?"

"No stop worrying Izzy. I don't need to leave my cottage there are opportunities close by. In fact, Danny and I were talking about this the other day. He feels that if we could find a suitable airfield to work from, it would be nice to get involved in transporting donated organs for transplant. Now with more sharing of transplant data with the rise of computers, suitable donor organs are being transported all over the world, but it is imperative that the donor organ is transported quickly and safely to the recipient. Therefore we both feel that offering a dedicated organ transport service would be a fulfilling role to play.

One of Danny's sisters needed a kidney transplant a few years ago and although she was lucky and there was a suitable match within the family, often there is not so the transplant team have to look further afield. If our idea took off we would be able to offer the transplant teams the chance to look worldwide for a suitable match. We have already approached the transplant teams to see if they would, in theory, use the service and have received an outstanding 'yes'. The training school we are with have a couple of aeroplanes that are still serviceable for use but which, as training aeroplanes, need to be decommissioned, so that leaves us with just needing a suitable airfield and storage for when the aeroplanes are not flying. Again the school has some spare land at the side so if we could get the funding to build a hanger, as well as purchase the aeroplanes, we might be able to set up the business. First of all though Danny and I have to qualify as pilots before we can investigate funding to begin the business. In fact Izzy, you might be interested to learn the aeroplane you flew in yesterday, is in fact, one of the aeroplanes due for decommission, along with the aeroplane that Danny regularly uses. This is the reason we both felt it was a fitting tribute to our aeroplanes to purchase them and allow them to continue to be of service to us and the world. The transplant teams are looking at getting funding and sponsorships together for us too so the next few months could be a very exciting but stressful time. I think, having you and the other fairies and elves from Penny's Kingdom, could be a welcome relief, and getting the garden prepared for the winter for you all, will be a welcome distraction from business plans, funding circles, sponsorship forms and such like." laughed Penny. "Now to attend to this tiny matter of enlarging this hole for you Izzy before I go off and continue with my training schedule. I wonder what I can use, as at present I don't want to make the hole too big to let the drafts in, but just big enough so you can pop in and out easily. Once I have made the door then I can use a small saw to make the doorway larger, as the door will stop any drafts. I wonder if I can use a screwdriver, just to increase the size by a little bit, as I have one here in the kitchen drawer. All my other tools are in the shed and I really do not have the time to go delving into my toolboxes."

Penny opened a drawer and took out a screwdriver and walked over to the back door. At the side of the pet door was a tiny hole about the size of a large pin head.

"Oh dear, I am so sorry Izzy, I did not realise the hole was so tiny! No wonder you had such a tight squeeze to get through this morning but unfortunately this screwdriver head is far too big to enlarge the hole. I wonder what else I can use instead, I wonder if the tip of the kitchen scissors would go in the hole instead?" mused Penny

Penny replaced the screwdriver in the drawer and opened another.

"Ah yes I think the point of these scissors might just go into the hole and then if I wiggle it a bit hopefully it will enlarge the hole."

Izzy flew down to see exactly what Penny was doing but Trixie did not want leaving out either, so she pushed her head up against Penny's hand. Just at that moment Dixie decided it was time to head out into the garden so popped through the pet door. As the door came back it hit Trixie on the bottom and with a yelp the puppy shot forwards dislodging the scissors not only from the hole but out of Penny's hand.

"For goodness sake you lot, no not you Izzy, before you go off in a huff, I am talking to Trixie and Dixie, get out of my way or this hole will never get enlarged!"

"I was not going to go off in a huff, thank you very much Penny," answered Izzy crossly. "I never go off in a huff!"

"Oh no," laughed Penny. "So why did you leave your orginal garden then?"

"I was fed up with the train if you don't mind," exclaimed Izzy. "Oh I see what you mean, so okay maybe

I was hasty, although look how it has all turned out in the end. Here I am living the dream with you, Trixie and Dixie in the most perfect garden and about to embark on my duties of the Fairy Queen of Penny's Kingdom. We ought to design an impressive entrance to the kingdom from the stream ready for the big national ball. I am sure with our joint creative design ideas we could make something extra special. What do you think Penny, can we do it?" asked Izzy.

"I imagine we can, but we have plenty of time to give it some thought, unless you want to put up something earlier so any visiting fairies, pixies and elves know where they have arrived at. If you are serious about exploring with me, and finding other fairies who live in different places like towns and cities, the seaside and the moors, then it might be nice to offer them the chance to visit your kingdom and get to know the area before the ball. That way they can help spread the word too. Mind you we would have to design some extra homes for them to stay in when they visit, like us humans have, when we go on holiday. We will have to make some fairy hotels and maybe something equivalent to our caravan parks, that type of thing."

"What on earth are caravan parks, I have never heard of them, or even hotels if I am honest?" asked Izzy.

"Oh I forgot you never travelled before you left home did you?" exclaimed Penny. "Well tonight, when I come home, I will show you some pictures of hotels and caravan parks on my computer or maybe some photographs, to give you some ideas to take to your subjects, as they might not want to share their garden with hoards of visiting fairies. In the meantime try out your new enlarged hole. It isn't big enough for you to walk or fly through yet, that will have to wait until I have made the door, but I hope I have made it big enough for you to crawl through. I need to think about lining the hole with something, maybe some type of metal with a rim on so I can attach the door to it, but as yet I am not sure what to use. Maybe something will come to mind in the next few days that I can use before I make the door at the weekend. Thinking about it, the door is going to be so tiny, only about the size of my thumb nail, and whatever wood I use it will have to be very light, or you won't be strong enough to open it. When my brother was young he used to use something called balsam wood, which was very soft and light, to make things from, but I am not too sure if you can still buy it now. I might ask Danny if he knows, because I believe he uses all types of bits of wood to carve shapes and animals. In fact, he might be able to carve you an unusual door from something he has at home."

"There you go again Penny you are determined to involve Danny in our adventures and things. Are you sure Danny will work with you and not laugh at you? I am scared he might hurt me if he knew about me," asked Izzy.

"No I don't think he would hurt you, remember if a human does not believe in fairies and elves, then they cannot see them. The danger lies in if they cannot see them then they can harm them accidently. Somehow I really think Danny does believe in them, but I will try and speak to him today and sort of test the water, by introducing the subject without telling him outright that you are living here. If Danny and I are going into business together, we will be spending a lot of time together setting it all up, so I would need to be sure you were safe anyway as I know what you are like, you would be so interested in all our plans," answered Penny. "Now try that hole for size as a temporary measure please Izzy."

Izzy flew over to the hole that Penny had enlarged and was able to fly straight through it without even folding her wings. She turned around and flew back into the house and landed on Penny's hand.

"Perfect Penny I can fly straight in and out without stopping thank you so much, I love you."

"Good and I love you too," laughed Penny. "Right time to drink my tea and set off for work as my instructor is accompanying me today to sign me off as completing my flying hours then I have other practical tests next week which involve maintenance tasks. If I pass all those, apart from maintaining my flying hours, the following two weeks will just be revision for my final exams, so I will be able to spend some time helping to get our garden, no sorry kingdom, ready for our local summer ball. Once Danny and I have finished our exams we will have to spend our time putting together our business plan, getting some funding to buy the aeroplanes and storage and launching the business so we can get the business established. Right now I know you are all sorted I will finish getting ready for work."

Penny quickly drank her tea and placed all her dirty pots in the dishwasher, collected her bag, keys and coat, gave Trixie a hug and left the house. Trixie bounded out of the house and watched Penny leave, like she always did, but this morning Penny could see Izzy perched on the top of her head. I hope Izzy will be alright today, mused Penny then shook her head, of course she would be okay, she was a fairy for heaven's sake, and had been looking after herself for years. With that thought lingering in her head she smiled to herself and set off for work. She was in a happy mood and was looking forward to seeing Danny. Now she had decided to tell him that she not only believed in fairies, but had actually one now living with her who had been made the Fairy Queen, she was looking forward to his reaction. The point was, if they were going to be business partners, then it was important that they did not have secrets from each other and this included, in Penny's eyes, the fact that she now worked with the fairies and elves of her kingdom. Penny was still in awe of all that had happened in the last 24 hours. Meanwhile back at Penny's house, Dixie was chasing butterflies and playing with a few young elves and fairies who were not yet ready for bed, and Trixie was snuffling about around the summerhouse. Izzy had popped under the house to check on the hedgehogs and see if they needed anything. All the hedgehogs appeared to be asleep but Izzy noticed the new hedgehog curled up close to Hetty's nest. Izzy smiled, it looked as if Hetty had got her wish and the lone male had taken up residence under Penny's summerhouse too, so that was another name Penny would have to think up! Actually he looked like a Hector to Izzy, so she would suggest that to Penny tonight. So Penny had two males and two females and five babies to name tonight. Izzy saw the expectant mum nestled in her new nest but then Izzy spotted that she wasn't actually asleep. Izzy tiptoed across,

"Are you okay I expected you to be all asleep?" she asked.

"Well I just finished my nest last night, and it looks as if it was just in time, as I think my babies will be born today. I feel so restless and uncomfortable."

"Oh my goodness I didn't realise it was going to be quite that soon Hetty said you expected to give birth in a few days not today. Is there anything I can do? Penny has gone to work, so I can't get her to help, you will have to make do with me until Penny gets back," exclaimed Izzy.

"No it is okay I don't need anything. It is lucky we managed to finish off the nest last night. The wind had blown in some soft wool, which had caught on a plant, so we lined the nest with that to make it cosy. I thought it would be a few more days yet, but apparently I was wrong, and it looks as though Penny will be having to find more names tonight," laughed the expectant mum. "Penny hasn't even given me a name, unlike Hetty, as she didn't know the rest of us were here."

"No she will have to get her thinking cap on when she comes home tonight," laughed Izzy. "She needs three male names, as I see the lone male appears to have taken up residence next to Hetty, two female names, five babies belonging to Hetty and however many babies you have. Penny's family is getting larger by the minute."

"Well I think it will continue to grow as Penny is obviously such a kind and lovely person and this garden is such a dream to live in. I am sure lots of the other wildlife will settle in or close by the garden. Did you know there was some water voles making homes along the bank of the stream behind the summerhouse? Technically I suppose it isn't actually in Penny's garden but in the forest but I imagine they will visit the garden frequently."

"Yes Mercury and the other fairies told us last night about the water voles. I was just on my way to see them but thought I would pop in and see you hedgehogs first," answered Izzy. "Any other animals already in residence I need to know about?"

"There are mice who have made nests under the patio. If you go to the bottom of the steps at the right hand side you will see they have gnawed a hole in the side of the step which leads to their homes actually under the patio. They were telling me a few days ago there was lots of room under there and yet they were safe from Penny's animals too. Maybe Penny might be able to give them some food like she does us?"

"I am sure she will once she knows they are there. Now I am going to leave you in peace but I might pop back later to make sure you are okay," Izzy told the hedgehog.

"Okay Izzy I might have some news for you by then. Off you go and visit the other residents I will be fine tucked up here in my nest. Oh by the way did you meet the forest fairies?"

"Oh gosh, yes we did, and they elected me their Fairy Queen with Penny as an honorary queen. The forest fairies are busy making the garden their kingdom headquarters and will prepare it ready for winter. They were going to hold a small summer ball anyway in four weeks time in the garden but we are going to create and promote a Winter National Ball here in the garden. Penny has lots of work to do over the summer and autumn to get the garden up to standard to hold a ball, but we felt that with us having the summerhouse here if it was too cold or snowy to have it in the open then we could use the summerhouse. This new kingdom is to be called Penny's Kingdom. I had forgotten we talked to you before we went into the forest."

"Oh my, that sounds wonderful and I am sure Penny

will be the perfect host, along with yourself, for the Winter Ball. How exciting to be part of this adventure. Let us know if any of us can be a help in any form, although I might not be much use for a few days until my new babies grow a bit."

"No problem," laughed Izzy. "You concentrate on your new role for a few days but you will be welcome to join us when you can. You may find lots of old pans and kettles appear hidden around the garden, ready for new homes for fairies and elves when Penny finds them for us. Penny and I will be on the lookout for other interesting things to use too on our travels as we intend to explore other different places and find elves and fairies who live in other communities. Now you rest and I am going to see the water voles and mice before exploring the forest some more."

"Don't get lost we need you Izzy," laughed the hedgehog.

Izzy flew out from under the summerhouse, and around the back of it, to the banks of the stream just beyond the fence, that separated Penny's garden from the forest. Here she found a tiny island, that the stream had made, on its way from two directions to form a single stream. One branch came from the direction of the waterfall, where Izzy and Penny had met the forest fairies, the other one from the forest at the side of Penny's house. Izzy guessed this was probably the part of the forest path that Penny had described, as the direction the dog walkers took, as there appeared to be a section of dense forest before you actually came to the clearing and waterfall, behind Penny's house. Izzy wasn't sure what this island could be used, for but she instinctively felt that it would play a significant part in her kingdom. She would have to bring Penny here and see if she could suggest a use for it. Maybe it could somehow be used for visiting fairies and elves to stay, now what had Penny suggested this morning, something about hotels and caravan parks? It was close enough to Penny's garden and thus the kingdom's headquarters for people to join in activities and access the kingdom but not directly in the kingdom so Izzy's subjects would not necessarily have to share their homes. Izzy fluttered down on to a small log to look at the island. In human terms it was not very big but in fairy terms, massive. Whilst Izzy was sat surveying the area she spotted a water vole coming down the stream with sticks and dried grass in its mouth. The water vole swam up to the bank in front of the log Izzy was sitting on.

"Hello there," called Izzy. "Are you building a home along the bank of the stream? I am Izzy, well to be honest as from last night, Queen Izzy and the hedgehogs were telling me there were water voles making homes in the bank."

"Well hello Queen Izzy, yes, there are now four of us living in these banks. It is the perfect spot, as no humans come to this side of the wood, apart from, occasionally, we see a human sat near the waterfall but she sits so still we do not feel threatened by her at all."

"That will be Penny, who I have come to live with in the dear little house at the top of the garden. She can see us all and talk to us and also can talk to the animals in her garden, so you will be quite safe in her company. You see the house there just over the fence, well that is a summerhouse in her garden and the hedgehogs live under there, so you can use that side of the bank too if you want. I was sitting here looking at that island created by the two branches converging and wondering if it would work to create some places for visiting fairies and elves to stay. I am not sure yet how it would work, I think I may have to persuade Penny to come and look at it and get her ideas. You see we are planning on making this kingdom another national base here in the north to rival the one right down in the south. Well to be honest that is my intention, I haven't raised the subject to Penny or my assistants Mercury, Topaz, Emerald or Sapphire yet. We have agreed to hold a Winter National Ball here in the garden to rival the Summer National Ball that is held in the south, so why not extend the idea to build this kingdom into another prestige centre for fairies and elves to stay when they are travelling to other kingdoms, or even just come and visit us so we can all swap ideas."

"Wow you certainly have ambition Queen Izzy but do you think it will work?" the water vole replied.

"I think so, especially now I have found the island. There is also the clearing in the forest in the area of the waterfall, that could possibly be utilised too. You know how fairies and elves love riding moonbeams and sunbeams made by cascading water, so the clearing could make another excellent extension to the garden. I think that my subjects, although happy to socialise and host fairies and elves from other places, they might enjoy the festivities more if they had their homes around the garden and the guests were accommodated outside the garden," answered Izzy.

"Yes I think you might have a point Izzy," replied the water vole. "It might get wearing after a time if you are constantly having strangers to stay in your homes. I think separate places for the guests to stay is an excellent idea. We, the water voles, would be happy to offer taxi services to any fairy or elf who wanted a ride from either the island or clearing to the garden as now we know who owns the garden we are not afraid to venture in there."

"Oh Penny would be delighted to see you in the stream in her garden anytime you want, although I suspect she will also want to name you too. She had already named Hetty, who was the first hedgehog to live in her garden, but last night she found out that Hetty had five babies and that there was also another two couples there too. Today I have found out a lone male, who used to visit, has taken up residence and that one of the female hedgehogs is about to give birth. The hedgehogs also told me there were mice living under the decked patio, so I am going to visit them today and see how many are there. But first I am going to investigate the forest a bit more. I want to see if I can find out more about the waterfall, see where it begins and things like that, as we did not get any further last night than the clearing. I also want to take a peep at the other side of that dense piece of forest where the stream comes from the other side and see what is over there."

"Be careful as there are often a lot of humans at the other side of the forest, where this branch of the stream comes from. That is why we are building our homes along this bank as there is no one in the area. We had occasionally caught a glimpse of Penny at the clearing but were unaware that we were so close to her garden. Now we know she is okay with animals around her garden, we can pop downstream into the garden to collect building supplies. It will be less hazardous than going upstream to the other side of the forest.

"Oh Penny would be delighted to allow you to use anything from the garden that you need to build your homes and please pop in and visit us, the fairies and elves of Penny's Kingdom, whenever you want. I promise I will be extremely careful if I venture to the other side of the forest. In fact, thinking about it, I might not even bother although I do want to explore the top of the waterfall and see what is beyond there."

"Oh you will be fine in that direction," answered the water vole. "The forest goes for miles in that direction before it borders farmland where there are cows and sheep. You would be flying for ages before you saw any houses or people. If you go downstream to the other side of Penny's garden you have not far to go across a field until you come to several houses and eventually a railway line."

"Oh thank you for that information. I wonder if the fields you are describing is where I met Tulip," mused Izzy.

"Tulip," queried the water vole. "Who is Tulip?"

"Ah, it is a long story. Now let me see I left home yesterday, no the day before, no I think it might have been the day before that even as I was bored with the garden we had always lived in and fed up of getting woke up every morning by the trains travelling on the railway, so I left to find my perfect garden to make my home in. I quickly grew tired and landed on the roof of a little house, that Penny says would be a dog kennel. Anyhow the occupant gave a mighty big snore and scared me to death. I screamed and woke the beast up and had to spend the rest of the day crouched behind the dog kennel."

"Why didn't you just fly away?" queried the water vole.

"Well as we didn't exercise enough, my wings had quickly become so tired I couldn't move them, and then it became daytime, so again I couldn't leave my hiding place until dusk. Believe me, I flew away so fast once it was dusk, to get away from the monster. Anyhow I flew quite a way again , well it felt like a long way, until my wings became tired so I landed on a rock in the middle of a field, only it wasn't a rock but a young calf called Tulip. Tulip allowed me to sleep tucked in beside her head for the night but then we had a dilemma as I couldn't fly during the daytime. Tulip suggested I climb up her face and into her ear so I was safe and warm for the day which is what I did and I had a wonderful day. At dusk I flew off again but this time I could fly longer as my wings were getting stronger. At daybreak I found a place to sleep but was soon awakened by someone invading my hiding place. I quickly found out that the human was Penny who believed in fairies and could see us and talk to us. I had, in fact, gone to sleep in an aeroplane so had a lovely time flying high up in the clouds. Eventually we finished our trip and I rode in Penny's pocket to the office, where I hid in a drawer until all the other pilots had left. When Penny and I were alone, I came out of my hiding place and told Penny my story. Penny offered me the chance to come and live with her and brought me here in her car. We passed a field with cows in and I asked Penny if she thought it might be the same herd as Tulip belonged to, but we didn't know how far I had travelled so didn't know. Penny said to go and explore and see if any of the herds were in fact Tulip's herd but I didn't realise if I went that way I would come to fields, then houses and then the railway track. It sounds as though that might have been the way I came but then how did I manage to find the airfield where the aeroplanes were?" asked Izzy.

"Oh that is easy. As you were flying away from the houses, across the fields where you met Tulip, you would go across roads and soon be at the airfield. If you actually followed the stream up there where people walk then you would in fact soon arrive on the outskirts of the airfield. I know because we used to live along the banks but people actually built houses over the top of the stream so we had to move. We have tried to build homes in lots of places along the banks of these streams but we have always became disturbed by people. Again we followed the stream to the other side of Penny's garden but the stream doesn't go very far after Penny's fence as it goes underground again with houses built on top. This piece of stream is the best place we have found, as we thought we might be able to use a bit of the other branch of the stream, towards the waterfall, where the water is still reasonably calm, if our numbers increased and we ran out of space. Now I know we can use the banks of the stream in Penny's garden too, I can see us having much bigger water vole community."

"Oh that is all so interesting I can't wait until Penny comes home tonight, I have so much to tell her. Well thanks for the chat. I may go the other way now and have a little peep at the field on the other side of Penny's fence, to see what I can see, before I fly up to the top of the waterfall and try to see how far I can see. Who knows if the waterfall is high enough I might see across the fields. I might actually be a lot closer living here, than I ever imagined to my old home. Although I can't be that close, as I never heard the train this morning."

"Oh no you wouldn't hear the train as the track is way over the fields and houses but as you can fly I imagine it wouldn't take you long to fly and visit your family. Now I must get on too. We will all definitely come and introduce ourselves to Penny one of these evenings and you enjoy your day exploring."

With a flick of his tail the water vole disappeared among the reeds lining the edge of the bank. Izzy also jumped up from her seat and unfolded her wings. After a few tentative stretches she fluttered away following the line of the stream towards the waterfall to begin her next adventure

The Waterfall

Izzy soon arrived at the clearing where Penny and her had found the forest fairies and elves playing last night. This morning there was an abundance of birds, butterflies and dragonflies around the pool at the base of the waterfall. Some of the birds were taking a bath, some sat around on stones drying their wings in the early morning sunshine. All were singing a joyful song and Izzy spied a few of her young subjects frolicking on the sunbeams. Izzy couldn't blame them, even though normally fairies and elves slept during the day. After all, Izzy was a fairy too, and she was still out and about. Izzy joined a couple of blue tits on a warm rock to take in the scene.

"Good morning," Izzy politely addressed the birds. "What a lovely morning and a special place this is," she continued. "I became Queen Izzy last night and met many of my subjects here. In fact there are a few of the younger members of our kingdom playing on the sunbeams."

"Oh we are very pleased to meet you Queen Izzy. The resident fairies and elves were telling us about you and Penny this morning when we awoke. We, and all the other birds here, live in and around Penny's garden but usually come here for a bath every morning in this natural pool. As we live in Penny's garden we knew she was a special person, but didn't realise until this morning, how special."

"Oh she is a super person and can actually talk to the animals in her garden too. Last night we met the hedgehogs and Penny found she could talk to them, and understand them when they talked to her. Obviously she can see and talk to us fairies and is going to help us get the garden ready for our summer ball then we are going to work on making the garden our kingdom headquarters. We are hoping to hold a Winter National Ball too so there will be a lot of activity in the garden over the next few months," answered Izzy.

"Yes Mercury and the others were telling us about your

plans this morning. They are all very excited about it all."

"Well I have just seen an island, behind Penny's summerhouse, that I think could be developed into extra accommodation for visiting fairies and elves and thought we might be able to use this clearing too. That way my subjects are not constantly turned out of their homes or having to share with strangers. After all, I am sure they will make excellent hosts and include the guests in their activities, but it might be nice to feel that the homes they have chosen and developed, are exclusively their own," explained Izzy.

"Now that sounds an excellent compromise," answered one of the birds. "We are happy to help in any way we can, just tell us what you need."

"Well we will be looking to line and insulate the resident's homes in the garden for a start, so anything you find would be appreciated. I am not actually sure how we will develop the guest accommodation at present. I will need to discuss it with Penny, as she might be able to come up with some ideas. This morning, before she went to work she was talking about something called hotels and caravan parks, but I haven't a clue what either of them are at present. She said she would look some pictures out for me tonight when she came home so I might have more ideas in the next few days."

"I am sorry Izzy, or should I say Queen Izzy, I have no idea what Penny is talking about either, but if she can talk to the hedgehogs, she should be able to talk to us too. If she is going to show pictures, why don't you call a meeting of the animals, birds, fairies and elves who live in Penny's garden or will do once the fairy homes are prepared, and we can all see what you and Penny are planning to do. That way we all feel part of the plans and can maybe offer to help in the things we can do."

"Excellent idea," exclaimed Izzy. "The problem is, I actually don't know which birds do live in Penny's garden. I saw a few this morning as they were waking up, but I wouldn't recognise any of them again. The animals aren't a problem as I have been talking to the hedgehogs and water voles this morning. The hedgehogs informed me that there are mice living under the patio, and how to find my way into their den, so I can call a meeting easily with them. I am not sure at the moment where Mercury, Topaz, Emerald or Sapphire are sleeping, but if I pinned a note to the jetty where the boats are moored, I could get a message to them as someone would see the note. That just leaves you birds. Do you know who lives in the garden?"

"Actually yes, we know most of them don't we dear?" one of the birds said. "Please meet my wife Izzy."

"Pleased to meet you," Izzy replied. "I know you two are blue tits and I spied a robin and blackbird this morning. Are there many others?"

"Well there are swallows and house martins nesting under the eaves of Penny's cottage and bats in her garage roof. We have a pair of robins, some blackbirds, sparrows, chaffinches and wrens that I know of," replied the male bird.

"Don't forget the jackdaws, thrushes and wagtails dear and the pair of magpies that frequently visit the garden," prompted the female.

"Wow so we have lots of birds too. This garden of Penny's just keeps on growing. When I came yesterday, I was enchanted by all the beautiful flowers and unspoilt wildness, but I never imagined there was so much wildlife already living here," burst out Izzy. "This is fantastic, oh I am so excited and to think I am Queen of all this, never mind all the plans Penny and I have made to learn about other fairy communities. Thank you for telling me all this, I am going off to explore the forest now, but I will be home long before dusk. I had better write the note for Mercury when I come back too."

"Well why don't you ask those young fairies and elves where Mercury and the other girls sleep, as you will no doubt need to know soon, while you get all your plans sorted?" answered the male blue tit.

"Now why didn't I think of that," laughed Izzy. "Fine

queen I am going to make if I can't see something so simple?"

"You are still new to the job and I know you are going to make an excellent queen," chided the female. "Do not be so hard on yourself. Now go and ask your subjects where you can find your deputies and we had better make tracks too, or the nest we are finishing off will not be ready for my eggs. Bye Queen Izzy we will see you as the sun begins to go down this evening. We will pass the information to any of the other birds we see during the day about the meeting. The message will soon get broadcast I promise."

"Bye you two see you later," answered Izzy.

The birds flew off to get on with their work and Izzy flew over to her young subjects who bowed to her respectfully.

"Please could you tell me where Mercury, Topaz, Emerald and Sapphire sleep during the day, as I need to set up a meeting of all the fairies, elves, birds and animals that live, or will be living, in Penny's garden when we have got the homes finished?"

"Of course Queen Izzy follow us please."

Izzy and four of her young subjects left the clearing and re-entered Penny's garden. The young subjects took Izzy to a small tree stump in the corner of the garden near to the fence. The young fairies beckoned for Izzy to follow them round the back and slipped under a leaf. There, in the base of the stump, was a tiny hole which the young fairies indicated to Izzy, then stepped back. Izzy peeped inside and there curled on their sides were her four deputies, sleeping soundly. Izzy placed a finger to her lips and tiptoed away from the hole and under the leaf then she addressed the young fairies.

"Thank you for showing me. I will come back later to talk to them as they are sleeping soundly at the moment. I am now going to explore the forest and fields a bit more and I will let you get back to your games."

"We will escort you back to the clearing if you wish

Queen Izzy as we are ready for bed ourselves now and we sleep under a rock close to the waterfall pool," the young subjects informed Izzy.

Izzy and her subjects quickly flew back to the clearing where Izzy wished the young fairies sweet dreams.

"Thank you Queen Izzy, goodnight," they chorused in unison as they slipped underneath a stone at the side of the waterfall pool and Izzy flew off to explore the waterfall more closely.

The Waterfall Cave

She began by flying around the back of the waterfall, as she knew that there were often little nooks and crannies that were warm and dry, that often made wonderful homes for fairies and elves. Sure enough, as she expected, she spied several of her subjects tucked into tiny crevices in the rock face but then, to her surprise, she spied a bit larger an opening. She flew down and landed on the protruding piece of rock at the entrance and peered inside. She found that it was a large round room. It was very dark but warm and dry. Izzy squealed with delight. It would make a wonderful banqueting hall and could also make a ballroom, when needed, if the tables were placed around the outside of the room to clear space in the centre for dancing. It would need some lighting, but Izzy thought her deputies might be able to come up with suggestions what to use for this purpose. Usually fairies and elves could persuade glow worms to light their outside parties, but Izzy didn't know if they could persuade glow worms to inhabit an inside space.

Izzy realised that her sheltered upbringing in the family garden had not prepared her for the practical problems that she may encounter whilst she built her new kingdom headquarters. She hoped desperately that her deputies had more experience of the outside world than her, because unfortunately this was one problem that Penny would be unable to help with. Penny's hand wouldn't fit through the opening of the fairy cave even if she could get behind the waterfall. Izzy realised that if her deputies couldn't offer any suggestions, then her and Penny would have to see if some of the other fairy communities could help. She wondered if any of the animals or birds of her kingdom might have ideas and decided to bring it up at the meeting tonight. With a last look around the fairy cave to commit it all to her memory she left the darkness and emerged out into the light again. When she left the opening of the cave and stood on the flat protruding rock that she had landed on when she arrived and looked around, she noticed that it had tiny fairy steps leading away from the cave down to the rocky outcrop at the side of the pool and moss surrounding it on the forest floor.

Izzy tripped down the steps quickly realising that she had the perfect setting for her banqueting hall/ballroom. If the steps were illuminated by a string of lights on both sides of the steps then around the mouth of the cave what a sight it would present to guests attending either a banqueting night or a ball. Maybe when other kingdom leaders visited her, she could organise a banquet or ball for them on their last evening. In fact it might be fun to have a banquet for specially invited guests to begin all the season balls, especially when it was the Winter National Ball. Izzy hoped that she could open the National Ball to any fairy or elf that wanted to attend, but felt it might be nice to offer a special banquet to all the visiting heads of other fairy kingdoms and their deputies to attend first before joining Izzy's own subjects and visiting fairies in the kingdom headquarters so Penny could attend too. If Penny could come up with a suggestion of how to accommodate the visiting fairies on the island, then it might be nice for the visiting dignitaries to travel upstream and alight at the bottom of the steps and be escorted up a light strewn staircase to be greeted at the door to the hall by Izzy and her deputies. Izzy clapped her hands in excitement. Yes, she could picture the scene in her mind, she just hoped that with the help of her subjects, both fairy and birds, oh and not forgetting the animals of her kingdom, she could portray exactly what she had in mind for this special fairy grotto. Another subject to introduce at her first kingdom meeting tonight.

With a final glance, Izzy fluttered away from the rock pool that was at the base of the waterfall, to the top of the waterfall to see if she could find out where the water emerged at the top. As she flew upwards she realised just how high it was where it emerged from the rock face. She continued to climb further towards what she imagined would be the top of the rock where she could see an area of greenery. To her surprise, she found that the area was in fact another larger pond that was sparkling in the spring sunshine. To the rear was a coppice of trees and as she fluttered down on to a beautiful white flower to survey the scene, she was surprised to witness a female deer step delicately from the coppice of trees and tottering behind its mum was a baby. It was a bit unsteady on its feet so Izzy imagined he was only a few days old, maybe less. Its mum quietly approached the water and took a long drink. Just then another five deer emerged from the trees with three little babies bounding at their side, none quite as young or unsteady, as the initial one had been. All the adults proceeded to drink deeply from the pool whilst keeping a close eye on their offspring. The young deer soon began to cavort in the grass surrounding the pool kicking up their heels and chasing each other. The new born baby deer kept very close to its mother, peeping out at the other young deer, from behind its mum's back legs. Soon the three young deer had run off their initial high spirits and spied the new born baby. They bounded over to say hello and Izzy watched how they gently approached the baby so they did not frighten it. The baby shyly stretched its neck out to the older ones and touched noses with each in turn. The older ones then took a few steps away before turning around again.

"Come on baby, come and play," they chorused.

The baby dived back under its mummy's tummy before peeping out again. The older ones came back again to encourage the new baby to come out from under its mummy's tummy.

"Come on, come and play with us. We promise to be gentle," encouraged one of the older ones. "My name is Sally and this is Kenny nearest to me. The one hiding behind Kenny is Amy. She is the scared one."

"I am not scared, but I just don't want to frighten the little baby by pushing in too close. I am not like you two, I don't push myself forward. Hello little one, what is your name? You look as though you haven't been born long. How old are you?" asked Amy.

The baby's mummy looked up.

"Oh hello Amy, sorry I didn't see you. I was desperate or a drink. This is Benny and he is only 2 days old. He was born in the undergrowth just over there, so he was soon able to come with me to the pond. Benny, say hello to Amy, oh and I see you have met up with the twins, Sally and Kenny too. I don't think Benny will be able to come and play just yet he is still a bit unsteady on his legs, but give him a day or two and he will be chasing you over the meadow."

Just at that moment poor little Benny's legs gave way and he plopped down on the grass under his mummy's tummy. His mummy delicately stepped over him and continued to nibble at the grass near the edge of the pond. Sally and Kenny ran off to continue with their game of chase, but Amy slowly approached Benny. She gently touched his nose again, then slowly lowered herself on to the grass near to him.

"It's okay Benny to feel a bit scared. It is such a big world when you come out of the undergrowth, but you are quite safe here. We never see any people up here but there is plenty of food for our mothers. When we get a bit bigger our mummies will take us down the hill into the big forest, my mummy was telling me the other day. Providing we stay close to the waterfall that tumbles over the hill we are safe because there are no humans that go there. Only fairies, elves and lots of other animals can get into the clearing."

Izzy realised that these deer were in fact some more of her subjects who had come up to the coppice to give birth to their babies but would be joining her kingdom once the babies were a bit bigger. She unfolded her wings and stretched them slightly, before flying over to Amy and Benny.

"Hello Amy I am one of the fairies that your Mum was

74

telling you about, although I am now the queen and you, Sally, Kenny and little Benny too will be part of my kingdom. I was watching you all from that flower over there. Welcome to Penny's Kingdom and I will look forward to watching you grow. The fairies and elves will be living in Penny's garden which is the kingdom headquarters that is at the other side of the stream so you won't be able to actually join us in there, but I will look forward to seeing you at the base of the waterfall when you are strong enough to join us. By the way I am Izzy."

"Hello Izzy," Amy replied politely.

Benny's mummy and one of the other adult deer had heard the conversation too.

"Hello Izzy or rather Queen Izzy. I am Fern, Benny's mummy and this is Grace, Amy's mummy. Over there you have Candy, who is Sally and Kenny's mum, and Tina, Tara and Tammy who are sisters. Tina and Tara are waiting to have their babies but Tammy is too young this year, so it will be a while before we can travel down the hill to our autumn grazing, which is in the forest around the base of the waterfall. In fact we use the pool that the waterfall feeds as our drinking hole. We knew that there were a number of fairies and elves who lived around the waterfall, but we didn't know they had a Queen."

"Well to be honest they didn't until last night when they elected me their Queen," laughed Izzy. "I met Penny yesterday who owns the cottage with the beautiful fairy garden that is close to the clearing and we met Mercury, Topaz, Emerald and Sapphire who have become my deputies and they elected me their queen. Penny is wonderful, not only can she see and talk to us fairies, she can also talk and hear animals too."

"Oh occasionally we see a human sitting quietly on the rocks in the clearing next to the waterfall, but we have never emerged from the trees when she was there so we didn't know she had the gift of hearing and speaking to us animals. I wish we had known before as we could have come for a drink when she was there and introduced ourselves. Unfortunately now we will not be back down there until our babies have grown a bit, but if she wishes, you can bring her up here to meet us all. There are another five females and our husband who also live in the forest and up here during the summer. Some of us move down the hill into the lower forest for winter as it is far too cold this high up then, but we all come up to the coppice to have our babies. It is a much safer place when they are tiny and unsteady on their feet. We have this drinking pool on hand and this field extends around the coppice and down the hill on the other side so there is plenty of grass to eat for us as the field is too steep for anything but goats or sheep which are cloven hoofed animals like us."

"Lovely to meet you Fern and Grace. I had not realised my kingdom would have so many different animals too. We have hedgehogs and mice living in the garden, bats in the garage roof and a variety of birds nesting under the eaves of the cottage, water voles making homes in the banks of the stream behind the summer house and now all you deer in the forest in winter. I wonder what else I will find in the area?" observed Izzy.

"Well there are lots of rabbits who live both in the coppice and the forest as they graze the field along with us. It is a wonder there are not some playing or eating here at the moment as there usually is! Then you have badgers, quite a few of them live deeper in the forest away from the waterfall, and there are two or three fox families around. Just before Benny was born I came for a late drink in the pool and I met a mother fox with four cubs chasing each other over there," answered Fern pointing away from the top of the waterfall. "I imagine her den is away at the other side of the coppice, which was why I chose this part of the coppice to give birth to Benny. Amy was born in this part too, but Sally and Kenny were born deeper in the forest. We usually try to have our babies in the undergrowth either at the edge of this drinking pool or around the edge of the clearing in the centre of the coppice. This area has the advantage of being closer to the water so the mothers can get a drink when our babies are younger but the clearing is much nearer the grazing so we can feed when they are young. This is the first day that Candy has been able to bring Sally and Kenny to this large watering hole and the reason they are much older. Amy is about 10 days older than Benny but she has been coming here since she was a few days old same as Benny. I knew Grace was going to the clearing today to see how Candy and the others were doing, which is why they all came together."

"How wonderful, what about the other deer you mentioned, have they had their babies yet?" asked Izzy.

"I don't know I haven't seen anyone for a few days but some of the others might know. Hey Candy, Tina, Tara and Tammy come over here and meet Izzy who is queen of our woodland fairies," instructed Fern.

The others wandered over to where Fern, Grace, Amy, Benny and Izzy were. Fern bent her head so Izzy could climb up on to her nose.

"You may as well save your energy Queen Izzy. I know you can fly, but as I am here you might as well hop onto my nose then I can lift you up to be level with us all. Don't worry about Benny, Amy will see to him, she has been looking after him while we have been talking although you may not have noticed it. He won't go far as his little legs are not strong enough to do much yet but you will see him get stronger every day now if you come up and see us. Izzy was just asking if any of the other females have babies yet," informed Fern. "I don't know as I haven't seen anyone for a few days."

"Well you have been rather busy lately Fern so we didn't disturb you. Grace was telling me you had had a baby boy. Welcome to Benny and welcome to the forest Queen Izzy," replied Candy.

"Thank you. I hadn't realised how many animals and birds inhabited the area around the waterfall and Penny's garden. I feel as if I have stepped into my own dream and I will wake up and be back in my boring home garden," laughed Izzy. "When I set off a few days ago to search for my perfect garden I never imagined I would have so many wonderful adventures."

One of the deer reached out and playfully blew down her nose at Izzy sat on Fern's nose.

"Oh don't blow me off whichever you are! Now each of you come and introduce yourselves and I will try to learn who you all are. At the moment you all look alike to me but I am sure you aren't."

The female who had blown at Izzy inclined her head.

"Hello Izzy I am Tammy I have a white star here on my face between my eyes so that might help you. Look, if you check my face and then Fern's you can see my star."

"Rubbish Tammy," Fern replied. "It is not a star, merely a white dot, but I will agree none of the other females in the herd have a white dot. You are also the mischievous one. If anyone is playing a prank it will be you. Beware Izzy watch this one closely."

"Actually Amy has the same white patch as you Tammy, but if you look but her patch it is as big as yours now, so I imagine it will be much bigger when she has grown. Hi Izzy I am Grace, Amy's Mum," the deer informed Izzy quietly. "I am not sure if I have any distinguishing marks but you are welcome to look to see if you can see anything."

Grace held her nose close to Izzy and Izzy transferred herself onto Grace' nose.

"Oh that tickles Izzy. Fern, how did you manage not to twitch when Izzy was sat right on the top of your nose end?"

"Well it didn't tickle my nose Grace," Fern replied. "Your nose must be more sensitive. Yes looking at Amy she has a large white spot, well actually her spot looks more like a star than Tammy's, right in the middle of her forehead. I had never even noticed before! It just goes to show how observant we all are of each other. Turn around Grace, slowly so Izzy doesn't fall off. Come on girls we are on the hunt for something on Grace's body that Izzy can use to identify her."

The other deer crowded round Grace and Izzy.

"There you are Izzy come and look Grace has a much larger white spot on the top of her tail. Oh and Tina you have a crinkly ear so that identifies you too. Hi Izzy I am Tara, can you see the larger spot? Look if we all point our bottoms towards you, can you see the difference?"

"Oh brilliant Tara, yes I can. Tina turn around again, let me see this crinkly ear. Oh perfect now I just have to work something different to look out for on you Fern and Tara and Candy then I have you sussed. What about the other five females, how do I identify them though?" answered Izzy.

"Well to be honest, although we share a husband, they don't come to the waterfall much where you fairies hang out. There is a small pond near the edge of the forest at the other side and we rarely see them in, what we term, as our patch," answered Fern. "Do any of us know if they have given birth yet?

"Three out of the five have," Tina piped up. "They are just expecting one more and then they have finished. The other one is like Tammy, too young this year to have a baby."

"Oh do you mean you are younger than Tina and Tara then Tammy?" asked Izzy.

"Yes," answered Fern. "I had Tina and Tara two years ago so they will be able to have babies this year. Tammy was my baby last year. Grace joined us last year from another herd along with Candy and Amy is her first baby. Sally and Kenny are Candy's first babies too, which is unusual, as we don't usually have twins as our first babies. We changed husbands last summer as our old husband got sick and died so all the girls could stay with us. So everyone, have either me, Tara or Candy got anything that Izzy can see clearly to work out who is who?"

"Come here Mum, let me have a closer look," instructed Tammy. "Yes I thought so, Mum your white patch is actually on the top of your back, right in the middle. Here Izzy hop on to my nose, I promise I will be good and not blow you off, and I will show you what I mean about the big patch of white on my Mum's back. It looks as if we all have a bigger white patch somewhere on our bodies but we have never actually realised it until we have had to help Izzy identify us all individually."

"Wow yes! You have a really big patch in the centre of your back Fern," shrieked Izzy.

"Well if it is in the centre of my back I wouldn't have been able to see it so that is why I didn't know about it," answered Fern.

"Now we just have to see where Tara and Candy have their larger patches of white now."

"I can see Tara's patch clearly now I know what I am looking for, it is on her shoulder, on the left side. Turn around slowly Tara, let me see if you have one at the other side. Yes, look everyone Tara actually has a matching pair of large white patches, one on each shoulder. That makes it easier as I know whichever side I am looking at, Tara has a white patch on her shoulder. That just leaves you Candy, oh and Sally, Kenny and wee Benny. I know I can tell Benny at the moment, but he will soon outgrow his spindly legs, so I need to know how to tell him, Kenny and Sally apart. I know we have identified Amy already but I need to know all the young ones as well as you adults."

"Well of course you do as we still have both Tina and Tara to have babies yet too so that will make at least six babies this year who will be spending the winter in the forest around the waterfall. Maybe more if either Tina or Tara have twins," answered Candy. "After all I have had twins this year and you had twins 2 years ago Fern. Now come on the rest of you, where is my large white spot?"

Suddenly Amy looked up from her spot next to Benny.

"Your spot is on your chest Aunty Candy between your front legs," offered Amy.

"Gosh yes so it is," answered Fern. "How did we all miss that?"

"Well I have had to learn to tell you all apart these last few days and I noticed Sally and Kenny's mummy had a white patch on her chest. Sally has a large white patch on her bottom. Not like Aunt Grace, whose patch is in front of her tail more on her back, but actually on her bottom. I haven't noticed any large patches on Kenny though. Maybe he hasn't any," answered Amy.

"Well providing the rest of the babies have something different on their bodies then I will know that Kenny is the one with no identifying marks," pointed out Izzy.

"True," answered Fern. "But what about Benny? We need to take a good look at him when he wakes up."

Just at that moment Sally and Kenny ran up to the group of adults.

"Sally, Kenny come and say hello to our woodland Fairy Queen Izzy. She is the Queen of the fairies who live near the waterfall where we spend the winter. I know you haven't been there yet but we will be going down there in the autumn. In the meantime Izzy and her friend Penny may visit us up here in our summer residence. Now stand still you two for a few minutes while Izzy checks you out for distinguishing marks so she can tell everyone apart. Okay, I see what you mean about Sally having a large white patch on her bottom. Can you see what Amy means Izzy?"

"Yes Sally is very easy to spot but is Amy right about Kenny, has he anything I can use to identify him by?"

Izzy fluttered down off the top of Tammy's head and slowly flew around Kenny. She couldn't see anything on his head or back so she flew a bit lower.

"Perfect," she exclaimed when she flew near Kenny's front legs. "Kenny has two large white patches on his knees. You missed that Amy! Right just Benny to go now until the new babies are born."

"Well done Izzy, so now you know who we all are," laughed Tammy.

Just at that moment Benny woke up and stood up. As he stretched he overbalanced and fell down again. Fern trotted over to her baby and nudged him with her nose.

"Come on Benny, try again," she quietly encouraged

him. "You can do it."

Benny tried again and this time managed to stay upright on his legs.

"Well done each time you try to stand it will get easier," his mum promised. "Quick now all have a quick look at him while he is standing," urged Fern.

All the deer and Izzy had a good look at little Benny but couldn't spot anything.

"It looks as if Benny has no distinguishing marks at all," the older deer observed. "Can you see anything Izzy?"

"No nothing I am afraid, so let us hope your babies have something I can use Tara and Tina or else I will be in trouble," laughed Izzy. "Mind you I have several baby hedgehogs and mice that I will need to try to sort too as well as all my subjects so this may take me quite some time to get it all right."

Benny nuzzled under his Mummy's tummy as he was feeling a bit hungry and Amy ran off to join Sally and Kenny in a game.

"Well goodbye for now Izzy" Tammy, Tara and Tina chorused. "We are going to have our breakfast. Is anybody else coming?"

"No, me and Grace will stay with Fern and our offspring for a while," answered Candy.

"Well I must be off too," Izzy said. "I still have lots to explore but thank you so much for teaching me who you all are. I will definitely try and get Penny to come up here sometime soon. Meanwhile I will pop up again in a few days to see if there have been any more babies born."

"You will always be welcome Izzy. If we aren't here then we might be at the other side of the coppice of trees, or failing that come to the clearing in the centre as we are often there, especially if it is a bit windy as it is more sheltered. Just come and explore the woods whenever you want. I am sure you will met many more animals here," answered Fern.

"I am sure I will and take care of yourselves. I can't

wait to tell Penny tonight about you all."

With a final wave Izzy flew off to the other side of the lake to continue with her exploring. She felt so lucky to have met up with the deer and so excited to tell Penny all about her adventures and all she had learnt today when Penny came home from work. In the meantime she intended to explore the other side of the waterfall on her way down to the forest floor to see what other animals or birds she might encounter on her travels or other interesting landmarks. After all she had already found a fairy cave and island so she was sure there must be lots more to discover.

The Wild Goats

As Izzy flew over the lake she saw how big the coppice actually was! In fact it was so big that Izzy felt sure it could be called a forest. She knew she hadn't neither the time nor the energy to fully explore it today, but vowed she would come back another day to investigate how many other animals lived there, apart from the deer that she had already met. She also made a promise to herself she would bring Penny up to the lake at the top of the waterfall, but was aware they would have to walk through the forest to the other side before climbing up through the field the deer had mentioned, to the other side of the coppice. Izzy wasn't sure how long it would take to do all that, but guessed they would have to do it some day when Penny was not at work. In the meantime she wanted to see what was over the other side of the waterfall and where it led. Having found an island in the stream behind the summer house and then the banqueting hall/ballroom and steps leading to it from the forest floor she was now excited to discover more about her kingdom.

Izzy found that the ground fell sharply on the other side of the lake. The ground was very rocky too with very little grass growing on the hillside, and what was growing was very tough and coarse. She fluttered over the ground encountering several butterflies flitting around and quite a few bumblebees gathering pollen and nectar on their travels. She suddenly stopped dead in her tracks as she encountered the most extraordinary animal she had ever seen. She plumped down on a large rock to watch it. Izzy's eyes got wider as she saw several more of the strange animals emerge over the brow of the hill. They seemed quite happy eating the rough course grass that was managing to grow on the rocky ground. The one that appeared to be the leader had two huge horns sticking straight up. The others had the same type of horns but not as large as the leader. All of them munched delicately at the grass but what fascinated Izzy the most, was the way they scrambled over the rocks, occasionally having to sort of hop over the larger rocks. Izzy watched them for quite a while, trying to decipher what these strange animals could be. She had never in her life encountered anything like them but to be honest she didn't have a massive knowledge of animals. She decided she was going to have to fly over and ask these strange animals exactly what they were, but the leader with the huge horns looked so scary she was really nervous. It didn't help that as well as the big horns he had a long beard hanging from his chin and tiny eyes that made him look almost evil. His coat was long and shaggy, some patches hanging off as though he might have caught it on branches or thorny vegetation. There were bits of twigs and plants stuck in it which all added up to his general wild appearance.

Gathering up all her courage Izzy left her rocky perch and flew over to the shaggy beast. Somehow she knew instinctively that this was the leader of the herd and that she needed to make his acquaintance. She wasn't too sure if the herd was actually part of her kingdom but somehow she felt they were wild and didn't actually belong to anyone. She briefly wondered where they actually lived as she didn't feel that their home was this exposed, rocky outcrop but she was mystified where else they might live. With much trepidation she flew over to the scary beast and addressed him in a high scared voice,

"Hello my name is Izzy, I am the queen of the woodland fairies down on the forest floor near the base of the waterfall. Would you please tell me what kind of animal you are because I have never seen one like you before and also can you explain where you live?"

The animal looked up from where he was grazing and Izzy gulped as he looked even more scary close up.

"Well hello Izzy," he replied in a deep gruff voice. "I am a male wild goat which is called a billy. My name is Bertie and these others grazing the waterfall side are my wives. We spend the summer mainly on the rocky side of the waterfall as there are several crevices that we can shelter in during the night or if it is particularly wet and windy but our winters are spent in the forest around the waterfall. There is plenty of shelter and food in the forest for us all and no one bothers us as we are very shy creatures. If you are the queen of the fairies then I guess you are our queen too."

"Oh how super I have never seen a wild goat before in fact I didn't know there was such an animal. I can see how your coat will blend into the forest floor especially in winter but also if you are laid on the rocky sides of the waterfall you will blend into the grey of the rocks and crevices. I have already met the family of deer that winter down in the forest around the waterfall a few minutes ago so meeting you too is so wonderful. Just wait until I tell Penny about all the different animals and birds that are either presently living there or will be joining us in the autumn and winter."

"Who is Penny?" asked Bertie.

"Penny is the wonderful lady who found me and brought me to live with her. She lives in the cottage near the waterfall and can see and talk to the fairies, elves and animals. Well as yet she has only been talking to the animals in her garden as she hasn't been out and about with me today. The deer that come to the waterfall had seen Penny sitting on the rocks around the waterfall before but hadn't emerged when she was there. They have promised that in future they will not be so shy, although I am hoping to find a way up to the coppice so Penny can meet the deer before the autumn," answered Izzy.

"Oh we have also spied a woman sat on the rocks near the waterfall but like the deer didn't allow her to see us. If she has the special gift of talking to the animals then we will be happy to come and meet her. We can soon skip down and see you all within the next few weeks as our new babies are strong enough now to go on a little trip unlike the deer as their babies are still very young," explained Bertie.

"You will be most welcome to come and say hello. Unfortunately, like the deer, you won't be able to visit us in the garden although I might be able to persuade Penny to remove the gate at the woodland side of the bridge so more of the woodland animals can come and visit us in the garden. After all if the bridge is strong enough for Penny to cross the stream I am sure it will be strong for most of you animals providing you don't all decide to come at once," laughed Izzy. "Our kingdom is called 'Penny's Kingdom' and we are planning on organising a Winter National Fairy Ball in Penny's garden. We are going to have a small local summer ball in four weeks then a bigger one for autumn before going for the large one in winter."

"Oh how exciting the fairies will love that as I know they have been planning on expanding into the garden over the stream but were unsure of the owner of the cottage. We will certainly visit as close to her garden as we can but I don't think the garden will be large enough for all the woodland animals you are going to find that live in your kingdom. Well certainly not all at once anyway," laughed Bertie. "What I might do is bring one or two wives at a time if we are visiting. We will also have to make sure the deer are not visiting at the same time though."

"Oh I never thought about that. No the garden certainly is not big enough for more than two of you large animals at once so it might be better if we, that is Penny and me, meet up with you in the forest," answered Izzy.

"Well if you go to the bottom of the waterfall side and go around the back of the waterfall you will find yourself in a large clearing. No one ever goes into the clearing and you will find it is big enough for most, if not all of the animals in your kingdom, so it might be useful if you wanted to call a meeting anytime to discuss things," answered Bertie.

"Wow that is wonderful I will certainly go and explore it today as I need to call an emergency meeting of the birds and small animals that live in the garden as well as all the fairies and elves. This meeting is more about how to develop the garden into a great kingdom headquarters but we may need to call a bigger meeting if we intend to extend our ideas that might impact on the woodland animals too. For example while exploring behind the actual waterfall I found a perfect opening in the rock that will make a banqueting hall or even an intimate indoor ballroom. I need advice on how to light it but I am sure that either some of the fairies or elves in my kingdom will have the knowledge of how to do that. There was also a set of tiny steps leading from it to the ground which we could light and build a jetty at the bottom of the steps so visiting dignities can travel to the banquet by boat. At the moment I am not sure how to get the boats upstream but that is something I plan to add to the meeting tonight for suggestions."

"It sounds as though you have lots of ideas Izzy," laughed Bertie. "Unfortunately all us animals are too big to help with pulling fairy boats and things but maybe you could use mice or even birds to pull them along."

"What a good idea I never thought of that Bertie. The water voles also offered to be involved in a taxi service by offering rides on their backs for any fairy or elf that needed a lift so that is another suggestion. I know we have several families of mice who live under the patio in Penny's garden but as yet I haven't met them. I was going to see them after exploring the forest and waterfall. I had no idea that I would meet such a lot of interesting and friendly animals on my travels. In fact I will be honest and tell you now that I was terrified of you when I first saw you. You don't know how much courage it took to approach you but I am so glad I did. The deer were telling me that there are foxes, badgers and squirrels living in the coppice with them but I haven't explored that yet so I haven't met the animals," answered Izzy.

"Well if you pop over there to where my wives are grazing and say hello to them they will introduce you to all the rabbits that live on the other side of the waterfall where the land is less rocky so more grass grows. The rabbits are able to burrow underground round there. Technically, I suppose as the area belongs to a farmer, it is not your kingdom but the sheep that graze there do so all year and even have their babies up here. Over there is not so private so we seldom go as there are often humans walking across there but the rabbits join the sheep to eat. There are several rabbit families that live around the clearing as it is a large grassy area with lots of easy burrowing areas so you have a number of rabbits actually living in your kingdom," explained Bertie.

"That is brilliant thank you so much for all the information. I will pop over and have a quick visit to your wives and say hello to any rabbits that are there but if several humans are in the area I probably won't consider that area as part of my kingdom although that might be the way I bring Penny to explore the coppice with me as I am aware she can't fly to the top of the waterfall like I can," laughed Izzy.

"No Penny can't fly but if you take her through the forest on the right hand side of the waterfall she will come to the clearing and then it is a short climb through the trees before emerging on to this quite steep rocky part of the waterfall that you can see here," explained Bertie. "If Penny is reasonably fit she should be able to scramble up this part to the top of the waterfall. She can go the other way, but it is a much longer walk, as she has to walk right through the forest to the other side where she will pick up the footpath that winds across the open heath where the rabbits and sheep graze before reaching the coppice from the back. She will then have to find her way through the coppice to either the clearing or the lake where you have just seen the deer," instructed Bertie. "The point is there are some excellent paths through the forest especially after the clearing as they are the ones we have used for generations to connect this rocky summer grazing of ours to the clearing. We usually use the lake at the top of the waterfall for drinking in summer but when we move into the forest during autumn for the winter we use the waterfall pool for our drinking water hence the good paths."

"That sounds great Bertie, thank you so much. Yes Penny is definitely fit enough to climb up here I am sure especially on a nice sunny day but she might not manage it when it is wet and slippery."

"Oh no, please don't let her attempt it on wet days. Both me and my wives, as well as all the woodland animals, will be honoured to meet her and get to know her. When you know which day you are both coming I will pop down to the clearing and escort you on the best path to reach this area. As my wives and I have such strong horns we can, in the meantime, go down and clear the path of undergrowth, and any stray and broken branches on the trees, to make Penny an easy path to get on to this area and I will also try to investigate, and if necessary, clear a good pathway for Penny to use so you can both visit us all as much as possible over the summer."

"Oh Bertie, would you really do all that for us? You are so kind. The deer said we would have to go through the forest to the other side of the waterfall, why was that?" asked Izzy.

"Well probably because this is all too rocky and exposed for them to use to the forest especially when their babies are quite young. They use the other way going through the coppice which actually extends quite a way down the hillside, and then slipping quickly into the forest. Once they make the journey to the forest for winter during autumn they never return to the coppice until the following spring whereas we pop up and down the waterfall regularly all year whenever we feel like it. There are maybe two or three weeks after their babies are born when the mothers stay close to the sheltered areas but the babies soon become strong enough to run and play among the rocks and we can use both the forest and coppice and all the grazing between to live on," Bertie said.

"Ah, now I understand," replied Izzy. "Well it sounds as though Penny and I have lots of exploring to do over the next few months. Thank you so much for all your help Bertie. I will talk to Penny when she comes home tonight and find out when we can take you up on your offer of a guide through the forest to this area so we can go and visit the deer and maybe the rest of the animals who live in the coppice. Will it be alright if I pop back another day and tell you which day, weather permitting, when we will be coming? In the meantime I will say hello to your wives and their babies before making my way down the hillside and into the forest at the side of the waterfall and see if I can find the clearing you have been telling me about."

"I tell you what Izzy, perch yourself on the top of my head between my horns and I'll give you a lift. My horns will protect you as we go through the forest although as we scramble down the rocks you may have to hang on tightly to my coat," suggested Bertie.

"Wow that sounds like fun, the other day I spent the day riding in the ear of a calf as I had slept during the night so needed to wait until dusk before continuing on my travels. Tulip, that was the calf's name, offered me a hiding place for the day in her ear," Izzy told Bertie. "It was such fun as I could peep out whenever I wanted except when she, Tulip, put her head down to eat grass or suckle milk from her Mum then I had to hang on tight to the hair inside her ear."

"Well today you can explore the side of the waterfall, the forest, the clearing and when we have finished all that, I will give you a lift back through the forest to the waterfall. How does that all sound?" laughed Bertie.

"That sounds absolutely fine Bertie," replied Izzy. "I can then go back into the garden and meet the mice. I want to explore the garden a bit more so I have a clear idea of the layout of it before our meeting tonight and can put suggestions forward for discussion. I am sure over the next few weeks we will be calling a meeting of the animals in the forest. I am aware that the deer can't join us yet for a few months and until I meet the other animals from the coppice I am unsure if they will come down to the forest floor clearing so I might have to hold some meetings in the clearing at the top of the waterfall in the coppice but I will decide when I know more. I don't want the animals from the coppice to feel that they are being ignored especially as some of the deer and maybe other animals, like you and your wives, use both areas depending on the seasons."

"You may find that some of the birds use both the forest and coppice but apart from possibly the squirrels I think the animals will largely remain in either the forest or coppice. I know that you have foxes and badgers in the forest, definitely rabbits and squirrels and obviously mice and hedgehogs the same as in the coppice so you still have a range of animals without including those from the coppice. Do you know if you have fairies and elves living in or around the coppice too?" asked Bertie.

Izzy looked surprised.

"I don't know Bertie. No one has ever mentioned it. Surely if there was the deer would have mentioned it or the other fairies or elves last night?"

"Possibly but if they live deep in the coppice around the clearing then the fairies that you met last night might never have met them and there are only a few of the deer who come to the waterfall near Penny's cottage. Did you meet all the deer that live in the coppice this morning?" asked Bertie.

"Well no, I only met the ones that were drinking at the pool. They mentioned that there were other deer but that they seldom, if ever, came to the waterfall, so I would be unlikely to see them on a regular basis," replied Izzy.

"There you go then you might find that there are other fairies and elves living around the clearing in the coppice. The clearing is only small, well in comparison to the large clearing in the forest, with several small streams meandering through the trees and obviously no waterfall, but I guess there could possibly be some living there," suggested Bertie.

"Well I suppose so Bertie," mused Izzy. "I am sure that fairies and elves live in many different places and Penny and I are hoping to explore all types of areas to see if we can find fairies in them. You see Bertie, my family lived in the same garden for generations. It was such an immaculate garden, right next to the railway line and so boring, so three days ago I left home to find my perfect garden to make my home in and I have had such fantastic adventures and now live in Penny's house with her puppy and kitten, have the most wonderful garden to play in and have become a Fairy Queen with my very own kingdom. Occasionally, when I lived at home, a passing fairy would land in the garden en route to somewhere and describe their home and I would be so envious so now I am determined to encourage other fairies to visit us. I am not sure yet of the details but I want to have separate accommodation for visiting fairies and elves so that my subjects do not have to share or give up their homes once we get their permanent homes established in the garden. Penny is going to look for old pots and pans to hide amongst the flowers, under bushes or in the trees. We hope to be able to put lots of soft wool or fur inside for the fairies and elves to snuggle into especially during winter. While I was exploring this morning, I found that the stream from the waterfall met the stream from the forest and had formed an island behind Penny's summerhouse, so I want to show it to Penny and see if she thinks we could somehow use the island to build visiting fairy accommodation. Penny is great she can come up with such wonderful ideas so I am sure between us we can design something. That is what I am going to discuss at tonight's meeting along with ideas for the banqueting hall."

"All that sounds a wonderful idea. We might be able to help with the wool to line your houses and things. The birds often collect it off branches and bushes to line their nests in spring and this is just the same," answered Bertie.

"Penny mentioned something about collecting wool on our travels so if we have a constant supply here at home that saves us a job. I will certainly mention it to her and the rest at the meeting tonight," replied Izzy. "Now if I make myself comfortable maybe we can set off on our travels."

"Sounds like a plan Izzy," laughed Bertie. "Okay hop on board, your carriage awaits you Queen Izzy."

Izzy flew to the top of the goat's head and settled herself comfortably between his horns. She found that, to her surprise, it was a lovely soft cushion when she buried down underneath the longer coarse hair on the surface. The longer hair made a wonderful harness to cling to so she felt confident that she could fold and rest her wings whilst Bertie took her on a tour back to the clearing in the forest and then to the waterfall. She was so pleased she had actually plucked up the courage to speak to Bertie as he was really a kind and friendly animal.

"Okay Bertie I am settled and comfortable here between your horns. I have a wonderful view of where we are going so I should be able to bring Penny up here on the paths when we have time."

"Good off we go then," Bertie replied. "I will just introduce you to my wives first, because they all know the paths we use regularly and any of them will happily give you a ride to wherever you need to go, and then I will take you to see the clearing where many of us animals meet or live especially in winter. Hang on tight now until you get used to the motion of my head."

"I am hanging on tight, I promise," laughed Izzy, "but to be honest this bed I am sitting on is so comfortable I can bury my legs in so easily and just use a couple of strands of longer hair to use as a harness. I am confident I can fold my wings and relax which will let me have a rest as I have flown quite a lot today."

"Bertie at your service then madam," he laughed, "and off we go."

Bertie trotted gently across the rocky outcrop towards the other goats who were grazing on any grass they could find.

"Ladies please meet our forest Fairy Queen Izzy who was elected last night and took over her duties. She is exploring the kingdom and although technically our summer grazing doesn't encompass her kingdom she will be the queen over us during winter when we move permanently down into the forest. Right Izzy just briefly leave your comfortable bed and say hello to everyone and then you can snuggle back down again when we move off to our next destination. Ladies I am taking Izzy back down the rock side and along the paths to the clearing to see that and then take her from the clearing to the pool at the bottom of the waterfall," explained Bertie. "Izzy lives with the owner of the cottage that the fairies were planning on using the garden to extend their living quarters into. Most of us have sometimes seen a human lady sat quietly on the rocks next to the waterfall but of course never emerged from the trees when she was there. Izzy has been telling me that Penny, that is the woman's name, has the gift of communicating with animals as well as being able to see and speak to fairies and elves."

"Well to be honest, apart from me and the other fairies and elves and the hedgehog last night, who lives under the summerhouse, she has not practised talking to other animals. All that will change tonight as Hetty the hedgehog has babies and another of the females is about to give birth, probably today. I have learnt on my travels that we have water voles living and making homes along the banks of the stream, mice living under the patio, I haven't met them yet, lots of birds who are also looking for homes either in the garden or between the garden and the waterfall and the deer from the coppice who winter down in the forest. Bertie here assures me there are badgers, foxes, squirrels and rabbits who actually live in my kingdom as well as yourselves."

One of the ladies detached herself from the group of goats.

"Hello Queen Izzy and welcome from all us females. Any of us will be happy to give you a ride anytime you need one. I am Betty the matriarch of Bertie's harem. Most of the females are related in some way or another. Bertie joined us last year so all the babies are his. He had a fight with our old male, who was becoming quite sick, in the autumn and took over Billy's wives and children. That meant all the females that were born last year could stay in this herd. This allowed the herd the chance to more than double as we had a prominence of female kids last year. The females born this year will have to move away from us in two years time when they become mature enough to breed. There is always the odd unrelated male to start up a new dynasty. I and my sister Belinda began this dynasty with old Billy and then the odd stray female joined us as well as a few cousins. As I say all the females who were born before Bertie took over can stay with us and a few females who were Billy's daughters and grand-daughters drifted back to us when Bertie took over."

"Gosh I never thought how many interesting animals I would meet today," enthused Izzy. "Something similar had occurred with the deer I met earlier although the old male deer had become sick and died. The new male, who I haven't met yet, had brought his previous wives to join the herd but I think the deer who I didn't meet today were probably those. The ones I met were all very friendly and appeared to be related to each other."

"Yes often if a male brings several of his previous wives to join an established group you will find that they don't mix much. Although technically they are part of the male's harem you will see divisions occurring within the herd. The females tend to stick in their established groups and share the rearing of the babies in this group. Usually the same happens with the goats but Bertie was a young male who had not managed to form his own harem before having the fight with Billy. Bertie was not the first young male to fight old Billy over the last couple of years as he became weaker but was the one who managed to win the prolonged battle and take supremacy," explained the female who had introduced herself as Betty. "Belinda come over here and meet Queen Izzy who our Bertie has befriended. She has just become the queen of the forest fairies and elves who live around the base of the waterfall."

Another female joined Izzy, Bertie and Betty.

"Oh my goodness," laughed Izzy. "I now have the same dilemma that I had earlier on. How do I identify all you goats individually?"

"Well Bertie has a much longer beard than us females and thicker and stronger horns," laughed Belinda, "but how you manage to tell us females apart I am not sure. We have all grown up together so just know each other without having to think. Hello to you Queen Izzy I am sure we will see lots of you especially once the autumn and winter sets in as we need to move more into the forest then to find enough to eat."

"Please tell me what else you eat other than grass as I am completely ignorant about everything as I had never even heard of wild goats, never mind meeting any before today?" enquired Izzy. "Oh hang on a minute I have just spotted a big difference between Betty and you Belinda."

"Have you?" asked Betty. "Please tell us what is different as I don't know of anything."

"I know what Izzy has spotted," laughed Bertie. "How do you think I learnt to tell you apart when I first joined you. Old Billy wasn't going to help me after I had ousted him as leader so I just had to use my eyes and ears. Right quick lesson Izzy, yes as you have noticed Betty has one horn shorter than the other, I guess at some point, maybe when she was real young, she broke a piece off as it hasn't a point on and Belinda here has a large dent in the opposite horn to Betty down near her ear."

"Oh yes I had forgotten that Bertie," laughed Betty. "Yes you are right when me, Belinda and our cousin Beth were young and daft we used to copy the young males in their fighting games. This particular day I wasn't watching where I was going and ploughed headlong into a protruding piece of rock when Belinda or maybe Beth, I don't remember, side stepped my advance. I was always a bit of a tomboy when I was young."

"You still are the biggest tomboy of the females although I must say our Betsy is slowly taking over your mantle. You must be getting old sis!" laughed Belinda.

"Our Betty ploughed into the rock and broke off the tip of her horn and yes Betty, that particular day it was me who was playing with you but Beth was there too. I remember you just shook your head afterwards and carried on with the game. Do you remember there were some rabbits eating nearby and nearly had a heart attack when this piece of horn flew through the air and pierced the ground right in front of them?"

"Oh yes," exclaimed Betty, "I remember now. The piece of horn broke clean off and went sailing across the mountain side and came down, pointed end first, like a spear. The rabbits just stared in horror then ran back to their burrows and didn't come back out for the rest of the day. For days afterwards they emerged warily and it seemed to take ages before they ever recovered from their fright! Do you remember how you got the dent in your horn Belinda?"

"No I have no idea, do you Betty?"

"No to be honest I hadn't even realise you had a dent," replied Betty. "Okay then Bertie have the younger members of the herd any distinguishing marks that Izzy can use to identify us?"

"Well Betsy has a large chunk out of her horn about halfway down, probably done by the same type of incident as yours Betty, as if there is any friendly fighting going on or any death defying leaping involved, you can guarantee Betsy will be at the forefront. Your cousin Beth actually has one front leg that is white and the dark coarse hair never completely hides it."

"Has she?" chorused Belinda and Betty. "Hey Beth come over here we need to look at your leg."

One of the goats lifted her head up but then went back to eating.

"Beth come over here a minute. It is okay you won't starve for two minutes and the grass won't disappear into the ground either," instructed Betty. "Come on you can go back to your lunch in a minute."

Reluctantly the goat gave up easting and wandered over to Bertie, Izzy, Betty and Belinda continuously glancing over her shoulder as she came.

"Now Betty, why have you called me over? I had found a lovely lush patch of grass and now someone else will find it and eat it," wailed the new goat.

"Oh stop whingeing our Beth you are never happy unless you are complaining about something. Here let us have a look at your front legs. How clever you are Bertie I see what you mean! Beth meet Queen Izzy, leader of the waterfall fairies, she is exploring her kingdom and was asking how she could recognise us all as we all looked the same and Bertie has been pointing out all our different distinguishing features. Mine is the shortened horn without a point done that day years ago when we were young and I ploughed into the protruding piece of rock and knocked the top off my horn and it scared the rabbits nearby when it landed."

"Oh yes Betty that was a real laugh. You have never seen so many startled faces then a mass stampede to their burrows," observed Beth. "Our Betsy has a similar deformed horn but she only chipped a piece off the side of her horn not a full blown shearing off like you. So Bertie what sort of mark have I? I haven't ever damaged my horns or anything."

"That was why we called you over. Bertie here says you have a white front leg or it sounds as though it is much lighter in colour than the rest of us have. Oh yes I see what you mean Bertie one of her legs is much lighter in colour than the rest. I wouldn't go so far as saying it is exactly white but it is certainly not the dark grey of the rest of your coat."

Beth looked down at her legs.

"Why yes so it is I had never realised, so Belinda that leaves you. Oh I know you have a massive dent at the bottom of one of your horns. I can't remember though how it happened, can anyone else?"

"Yes," laughed Belinda. "I have just been informed by Bertie that I have a dent in a horn. I had no idea that I had one and neither Betty nor me have any idea how it might have happened. I guess we will just have to accept that I have a dented horn. Well we have sussed four of us for Izzy, Betty, Belinda, Betsy and me that only leaves the other two goats that are the same age as Betsy and then the other five girls that were born last year. Right Izzy apart from Betsy, who we know has a chip out of a horn, we have Babs and Becky who are the same age as Betsy and have had their first babies this year and then we have Brandy and Bonnie who are Belinda's twins born last spring, Beth's twins from last year Belle and Bev and my baby from last year Bea. This year we have had a mixture of girls and boys. Babs, Becky and Betsy all had one baby each which is quite normal for the first year and we have two boys and one girl from them. Betsy gave birth to Freddy and Babs to Fergal whereas Becky gave birth to Fay. I had twin girls again Fiona and Fran, Belinda had twin boys Fin and Felix and Beth gave birth to Frank and Felicity."

"Gosh is it normal to have twins then?" asked Izzy.

"Yes we often have twins except our first and often second babies who will usually be singles but by the third pregnancy twins is quite normal," answered Betty who appeared to be the main spokeswoman for the herd.

"So normally, for example this year's babies, do they stay with the family group and what happens when they can't?" queried Izzy.

"Well because the babies born this year into our herd that Bertie heads are Bertie's sons and daughters they will stay with us until they are nearly 2 years old and then the girls will either attach themselves to another herd headed by an unrelated male or form a new dynasty together with a young male. Our young males mature somewhere between two and three and will leave our particular group around this time, to either challenge an old male for the breeding rights to his harem, or seek out a group of females who have no male leader, either because their leader has died or sustained a bad injury or because they are a group of young females. More than likely Fay, Fiona, Fran and Felicity will begin their own new dynasty pairing up with a young male and girls the same age as them from other groups," explained Betty.

By this time Beth had scampered back to her patch of lush grass that she had been grazing on before and Belinda had also wandered off leaving Bertie, Izzy and Betty chatting.

"Betsy is a leader like you Betty," observed Bertie, "so although she can remain here with us I imagine she will go and lead the other girls to form her own group. The other girls, Babs and Becky, are more content and settled to allow you to be their leader very much like Beth and Belinda are. Betsy is a chip off the old block so feisty and daring like you I guess it is no coincident that she has a large chip out of a horn like you."

"I guess not," laughed Betty. "Do you want to come and meet the rest of the group Izzy if I can manage to round them all up?"

"Can we leave it for another day please Betty as I have met so many animals and new faces today I don't think I will remember you all?"

"Of course you can Izzy. I tell you what, I will round us all up, including our new babies and meet you in the clearing one day so you meet us all properly in a group. It is only our group who lives in the forest around the clearing and the waterfall so you need to get to know us all well. Maybe your friend Penny could join us too?" suggested Betty.

"Oh would you do that for Penny and me, that would be wonderful," exclaimed Izzy. "I will find out tonight from Penny when she can join us and pop back tomorrow and let you know. Would that be okay?"

"I tell you what Izzy, to save you flying all the way up here again, would you like me to meet you tomorrow in the clearing and you can tell me which day would suit you and Penny best to meet us all, then come back here and let Betty know. She is in charge of the females and children not me. I just protect them all from any danger," asked Bertie.

"Oh yes please Bertie that would be great. If the others don't come into the forest around the waterfall for winter where do they find their food? quizzed Izzy.

"Some winter in different areas in the coppice, some do come down into the forest but stay deep in the forest well away from the clearing and the waterfall. We tend to stay in our own groups, generally several females and one mature male. You will find we remain in the same area for both our summer grazing and our winter one. Like Betty was telling you, the young males and females remain with their family group until they reach breeding maturity. The young males are driven out of the family group by the mature male, who will spend the autumn in a number of fights with challenging males for the right to take over his herd of females and breed with them. This is what I did last autumn with old Billy, who had survived a number of challenges the year before including me, but last autumn I won the fight and although Billy staged a few attempts to re-establish his superiority, I continued to win the challenges until he gracefully retired to live quietly on the fringe of the forest. Unfortunately his many battles over the years and especially the ones last autumn had weakened him and during a prolonged bout of snow and freezing temperatures he died," explained Bertie.

"Oh how sad for him," wailed Izzy.

"That is the way we survive, only the strongest and fittest breed, this is how we ensure all our babies are strong and healthy," replied Betty. "It is no use giving birth to week and sickly babies or they will not survive the winter."

"No I suppose not," Izzy replied thoughtfully. "I guess that is the way all the animal kingdom lives and survives. I suppose that I did something similar. I left our garden where we had lived for generations and struck out on my own. I found the first day I quickly became tired as we never flew very far, everything we needed was just there in the garden. We lived on the same food and never challenged ourselves. I am still not as fit as my deputies are but I am determined to build up my stamina so I can be a hands on queen and lead my subjects well."

"With your sense of adventure and determination I am sure you will make an excellent queen," observed Bertie, "and we will be proud to honour and support you. I am sure your kingdom will be the best kingdom ever. What is it called, did you ever tell us?"

"No I don't think I did," laughed Izzy. "I was far too scared of you at first. The kingdom is to be called 'Penny's Kingdom' as my subjects elected Penny as an honorary queen. As we are using her garden as the kingdom headquarters and she is bringing her human expertise to the project we all felt it was a fitting tribute to name the kingdom after her."

"What a lovely idea. Well Queen Izzy of Penny's Kingdom shall we resume our journey down to the clearing and see what other animals we can find to introduce you to before I show you the way between the waterfall and the clearing?" asked Bertie.

"Yes Bertie that sounds like a plan," agreed Izzy. "I will just hop back into my seat and we continue with our journey. Goodbye Betty I will see you again real soon."

"Bye Izzy see you soon," chorused Betty and Belinda as they trotted off to continue feeding.

Izzy flew to the top of Bertie's head and resettled herself into her seat between his horns. She folded her wings and selected a few strands of Bertie's longer hair to use as handles.

"Are you ready Izzy?" enquired Bertie.

"Yes thank you Bertie," replied Izzy.

"Okay off we go then, hold on tight Izzy."

Bertie carefully picked his way down the waterfall side so he didn't dislodge his precious passenger. Soon Izzy spotted the edge of the forest and Bertie slipped into the trees where they were less dense. He quickly picked up the path he was looking for and although there were a few brambles and bushes along the edge of the path, Izzy could see it would be an easy path for Penny to use too if she wanted to visit the goats at their summer grazing. It would also make a brilliant short cut to visit the coppice and see the deer when their babies were too small to travel down into the forest. As they travelled down the path Izzy spied several tufts of white wool caught on the thorny branches of the brambles and bushes.

"Are these tufts of wool caught on the branches from you and the other goat's coats, Bertie?" asked Izzy.

"Yes this was what I was telling you about that the birds collect to line their nests. It is the same as what you are snuggled into on the top of my head. During the year, but especially early summer, we cast a lot of our coat to make way for a new thicker one ready for winter. As we brush past low branches of trees, thorny undergrowth and bushes we lose bits of our coat. Sometimes we will deliberately rub ourselves against the bark of a tree to rid ourselves of patches of loose coat. We also use pieces of protruding rocks to rub off our loose coat as it can feel quite itchy once it has become old and loses its waterproof content. This was what I was suggesting you collect, or get your subjects to collect, to line your homes as it will make them lovely and warm and soft for you to burrow in during cold winter days," explained Bertie.

"Wow yes I am lovely and warm with only my lower body snuggled in your coat Bertie," Izzy exclaimed with surprise. "Imagine lots of it lining old pots and pans dotted around the garden. They would be awesome homes for my subjects. Each fairy or elf could have an extra piece to make their duvet from as, generally, several will share a home. Those that have already made their homes in holes in trees or tucked into crevices in rocks could line their homes too with it. I imagine this was what Penny was suggesting using but she said we would have to collect it from fences from sheep on our travels."

"Yes," replied Bertie, "this would be similar to what Penny was suggesting using, only as she said, it would be caught on fences from sheep. I am sure your goats will be able to supply enough for your permanent homes without the birds having to go short. We would have to see if we could supply enough to furnish places for your visiting guests as it will depend how much you might need, but that is a discussion we can have with Penny and you later."

"Absolutely," cried Izzy. "As yet I have no idea what Penny meant when she was talking about hotels and holiday villages and neither have the birds I spoke to this morning. Penny said she would show me tonight when she came home, so that is why I have called a resident meeting tonight in the garden for the birds, animals, fairies and elves so we can discuss how we are going to provide homes for all of my subjects, how we are going to organise the layout of the headquarters. I also found a beautiful cave behind the waterfall itself that is dry and warm that I think will make a delightful banqueting hall or small ballroom. We need to get lights in and some tables and chairs and light the steps leading up to it but the access is fantastic as the overflow from the pool at the base of the waterfall forms a tiny stream that joins the larger stream that runs along the bottom of Penny's garden."

"I know the stream you mean and yes I know the tiny steps up the side of the actual waterfall. I have often wondered where it led."

"Well neither you goats, nor Penny, will be able to visit the cave," laughed Izzy, "but I can assure you there is one."

"No unfortunately that will be exclusively fairy and elf territory," observed Bertie. "Now Izzy we are nearly at the clearing. We approach it from the back, the path that leads to the waterfall is opposite. There are no paths to the left as that piece of forest joins the area where the dog walkers frequent and all the animals don't venture in that direction."

"Oh when we arrived at Penny's cottage we veered to the left of the road that Penny said only led to her cottage. She did mention something about the fact that the other road led to a car park and was popular with dog walkers," answered Izzy.

"Yes we knew that there was only access to the cottage in the forest, as we called it, but of course we were unaware that the owner was such a special person. When you go back towards Penny's garden from the waterfall, go and explore the forest at the other side of it, as that is the other way you can get up to the coppice where you met the deer earlier. You go through the trees and come out into fields that have sheep in them then head across the moorland that have a number of public footpaths criss-crossing before joining the trees of the coppice," suggested Bertie.

"Oh yes the deer were explaining that way. They said that was the way they came down into the forest in autumn," replied Izzy.

"Yes that is because they spend the spring and summer in and around the coppice then migrate down to the lower forest in autumn and spend the winter in the shelter. Well some of them do anyway, some stay in the coppice but deep in the forest. The group that come down here often join us in the clearing on nice days."

"That would be the group I met earlier then," explained Izzy. "They were telling me they were the ones that used the waterfall for drinking, which is why they had seen Penny sitting by the waterfall, but that the other group of deer didn't come down into the forest so there was no point introducing me to them."

"Yes that is like us, there is only my group who regularly trip up and down the waterfall side and into the clearing. The others head into the coppice instead of down to the forest floor.

Suddenly Bertie emerged from the trees and Izzy gave a gasp of pure delight. Bathed in the golden light of the afternoon sun was a beautiful clearing with several rabbits freely nibbling the lush grass. There was a family of fox cubs gambolling in the sun whilst their mum foraged in the long grass at the edge and kept a close eye on her offspring.

"Wow Bertie, what a perfect place for holding a full kingdom meeting if I need to later in the year," breathed Izzy. "I wasn't expecting such a large clearing. There will certainly be enough space for all you goats, deer, fairies and elves as well as the rabbits, foxes and badgers you mentioned. All the birds can perch in the trees and the fairies and elves on the lower branches. Are there any other animals I have forgotten?"

"The only one I can think of is the squirrels but they will probably either sit in the trees or they may use the tree stumps, as that is what they use as their tables to crack their nuts on. I am so happy it meets with your approval Queen Izzy," laughed Bertie.

"I knew there was animals called squirrels but I haven't ever seen any. What do they look like Bertie?" asked Izzy.

"I am sorry I forgot about them before," replied Bertie. "Squirrels live in trees, even building their nests high up in them, and scamper along branches and jump from tree to tree. They have long bushy tails. If you didn't live close to a forest you won't have seen any before but I know we have quite a few here. I am not sure if there are any in the coppice though."

"I don't care now about what lives in the coppice, there is such a variety living in and around this forest" answered Izzy. "I wonder if I would recognise a squirrel if I had to meet one despite your description Bertie. What colour are these mysterious creatures anyway?"

"They are an orange/red colour," answered Bertie. "Hang on a minute I will ask if there are any about within earshot and ask them to come and introduce themselves. Hey, are there any squirrels close by as I have our Fairy Queen of the waterfall here with me who has never seen a squirrel?"

Suddenly there was a flurry of activity high up in the

tree tops before these strange creatures ran down several tree trunks and landed on the ground close to where Bertie and Izzy were standing.

"Ah here you are Izzy your very own squirrel welcome committee. Mummy fox and rabbits come over too and meet Queen Izzy who was elected queen of the fairies last night and took up her duties. She lives with Penny who owns the lovely little cottage near to the waterfall where the fairies and elves were hoping to set up their headquarters in the garden. Penny is one of the special people who can talk and hear animals as well as see and talk to fairies and elves. Izzy found her way to the top of the waterfall and met our winter resident deer as well as stumbling on me and my wives. I have given her a lift down to show her this clearing and then I will show her the way back to the waterfall. Queen Izzy meet Mrs Fox, I am sorry I don't know your name, the squirrels and rabbits. Come forward in turn and introduce yourselves."

The mummy fox rounded up her cubs and trotted over to Bertie. Izzy flew down from the top of Bertie's head.

"Hello Queen Izzy, I am Carol and these are my babies Cathy, Mandy, Ruth and Paul. I am sorry but they are a bit shy. Come on children say hello to our Queen Izzy."

The fox cubs hung back behind their mum until suddenly one dived out and over to Izzy quickly followed by the other three. Next came a couple of squirrels closely followed by another three.

"Hello Queen Izzy, I am Gretel and this is Gordon then we have our three children Sam, Stu and Steph. We are pleased to meet you and welcome you to our forest."

"Well I am pleased to meet you all too. I never thought I would have so many different animals living in my kingdom. Hello rabbits, I am afraid there is no point in introducing yourselves individually yet as my head is spinning. I have met so many animals and I know I won't remember everyone so I will just say a collective hello and get to know you as I visit the clearing. I will be bringing Penny to meet you all eventually, and Betty is going to bring the female goats and young down when we can get it arranged. I am not sure which day yet, until Penny comes home from work tonight, and we can find out when she will be around but I promise it will be soon."

One of the rabbits stepped forward.

"That is alright Queen Izzy we understand perfectly. In the meantime welcome from us rabbits and if we can help with anything don't hesitate to ask."

"No I won't," answered Izzy, "but thank you for your welcome and thank you Bertie for making all this possible. I am not sure if I would have ventured this far away from the waterfall as I would have been frightened I might have encountered people."

"Well you managed to find your way to the top of the waterfall without my help," replied Bertie.

"But that wasn't a problem because I flew up and I was aware that no human could follow me up there. After speaking to the deer I was aware I was perfectly safe to explore down the waterfall side, as I knew the coppice and lake protected me from any human contact. Penny had already warned me about the dog walkers at this side of the waterfall, so I don't think I would have risked it unless I actually had Penny with me," explained Izzy.

"Oh I see, well I will take you on the path that leads directly to the waterfall from here and then you can show Penny the way. She may not know that this clearing is actually here if she hasn't explored the forest."

"Penny never said anything about the clearing and I got the impression that she had only explored as far as the waterfall. She might have taken Trixie the other way where the dog walkers go but I don't know."

"Who is Trixie?" asked Bertie.

"Oh sorry Trixie is Penny's puppy and she also has a kitten called Dixie," answered Izzy.

"Are you safe living with them? I thought the kitten especially might have chased you?"

"Well I was the same but both Trixie and Dixie accepted me at once. In fact Dixie was funny because she cupped her paws for me to sit in. When we met the fairies and elves last night they were telling us that Dixie goes out and plays with them in the garden, so although she was surprised to find me in the house, she knew how to play gently with me. Trixie and Dixie have a pet door to come and go as they please and Penny has made a tiny hole at the side a bit bigger so I can do the same until she designs me my very own door with a catch on and everything. In fact we are going to design it together before winter because Penny says she doesn't want any holes, even little ones, to let drafts in during winter."

"This Penny sounds a real treasure. I can't wait to meet her," replied Bertie.

"Oh she is so kind but fun too. I am sure you will all love her once you meet her. She really understands fairies and animals. She even has a collection of different fairy models on her windowsill at work, so I can go with her whenever I want as her work colleagues will just think I am a model if they can see me. I was always told that only children can see fairies but now I am not so sure, possibly there are more people like Penny. She says we are going on lots of adventures once she has finished her exams and can relax a bit. She says her and another colleague are looking at starting a business together when they both qualify as pilots. I am a bit nervous of this Danny person in case he can't see me and hurts me by accident but we will wait and see."

"It sounds as though you are going to have a very full life fulfilling your duties as the Fairy Queen, planning balls, building headquarters and homes for your subjects, going on adventures with Penny, playing with Trixie and Dixie, designing fairy doors and goodness knows what else," laughed Bertie.

"Oh my goodness when you put it like that Bertie, it does seem a rather full life. Who would have thought how much my life would change in a few short days. It seems like a lifetime ago since I left the family garden."

"Well it sounds as though you don't regret any of it

anyway Izzy. Come on hop on board my head again and we will wander back to the waterfall before I go back to my wives. Thank you squirrels and rabbits for welcoming Izzy. I am sure she will see you all again soon."

"Yes thank you all so much and Bertie is right, I will see you all again real soon."

Izzy flew back to her seat on Bertie's head and the animals dispersed back to the activities that they had been doing previously. Bertie set off down a path away from the clearing with Izzy now enjoying her unusual mode of transport.

The Thunderstorm

Soon Bertie emerged from the trees and Izzy realised she was, in fact, back at the very place she had begun exploring from earlier in the day which was at the base of the waterfall near the island where the water voles lived behind Penny's summer house. This was at the opposite side of the pool that the waterfall fed where Penny and Izzy had met the fairies and pixies at last night.

"Oh wow Bertie the clearing is so close to Penny's garden we can easily come and spend time with you all during winter when you live here. Do the deer use the clearing too?" asked Izzy.

"Yes there is a family group of deer who join us regularly in the clearing but I am not sure if it is the same ones who you met this morning Izzy. Did you find out their names and I can check if you want, or you can leave it until you bring Penny up to the pond at the top of the waterfall and I will arrange for Betty to bring our other females and babies to join you all and then if those deer don't know the clearing, I can tell them where it is?"

"The group of deer I met earlier said they were the only ones who used the waterfall so I guess those are the ones you and Betty often see in the clearing. The adults are Fern, Grace, Candy, Tina, Tara and Tammy and the babies are Sally, Kenny, Amy and a new baby called Benny," replied Izzy.

"Yes those are the ones we have met or rather I remember Fern as she seemed to be the lead. I recognise Grace and Candy as other names but at the moment I can't picture them. The other three you mentioned Tina, Tara and Tammy doesn't ring any bells," mused Bertie.

"Well Tina, Tara and Tammy wouldn't be adults last winter. In fact Tammy would only be a baby last winter as she is too young to have babies this year. Tina and Tara are waiting to give birth soon and these will be their first babies."

"Ah now I understand, yes there was one adult female last year and two younger ones that Fern seemed to be showing around and then three young ones," Bertie remarked.

"That would make sense as Grace and Candy joined Fern from another herd last summer so wouldn't know the area. Obviously Tina and Tara, who are Fern's twins from 2 years ago, will have come to the waterfall and forest since babies so they would know the place and Tammy would be a baby so would stay close to her mum."

"Yes I understand" replied Bertie. "Obviously last winter was my first time as the male leader of our family but Betty and the other females had already found the clearing with old Billy so showed me where it was. I was still learning the paths and got lost several times to, or from, the waterfall and I remember Fern showing me the way which is why I felt she was the leader."

"Well this year Grace and Candy have had babies, Grace gave birth to Amy a few days ago, but Candy had twins, Sally and Kenny, quite a while ago deep in the forest so today was her first time at the pool with her babies. Fern had just given birth to Benny a couple of days ago so he was very wobbly on his legs. Tina and Tara are expecting their first babies soon so that will make at least six babies added to the little herd this year."

"Wow, so that group is growing fast too like ours. Poor Izzy, you soon won't be able to keep track of all your animal subjects at this rate. No wonder you have decided to just concentrate on the ones who live around the clearing and waterfall, at least part of the year, because if you added the coppice animals in too you would never cope," laughed Bertie.

"No I wouldn't, I thought there was a lot to remember when I started this morning with hedgehogs and water voles, then I was informed mice also lived under the patio in Penny's garden, which as yet I haven't met, but then I find I have a herd of deer and wild goats, foxes, squirrels and rabbits, possibly badgers, but as yet we don't know, and a variety of birds. This kingdom of mine keeps on expanding at a rate of knots," exclaimed Izzy.

"Yes it does seem that way Izzy," laughed Bertie. "Well here you are back at the base of the waterfall and I guess that is the steps leading up to the cave you were telling me about is it Izzy?"

"Yes I need a string of lights on either side of the steps and some for the cave. This island here needs accommodation sorting for visiting fairies and elves to stay in, although as yet I don't know what to use as there are no plants or flowers here, only a few reeds growing on the side of the stream. I am hoping that Penny can offer some advice on that problem. The water voles offered to provide a taxi service if no one wanted to fly, which I thought sounded an excellent idea especially if other more formal fairy queens than me visited, or if they had their beautiful dresses on for a formal ball."

"Well it is nice if you can offer that service. I imagine it won't often occur but it was good of the water voles to offer to do that for you," replied Bertie.

"Yes it was Bertie. Well thank you so much for showing me the path to the clearing, and offering to come and escort me and Penny back through the forest to the waterfall side, when we want to visit the deer at their summer residence. I will chat to Penny tonight and fly up to see you and the deer tomorrow to tell you which day we can meet you all. Would Betty and you be able to bring the females and babies to the clearing to meet us both and the other animals there before showing us the way through the forest and the easiest path up the waterfall side to the top?" asked Izzy.

"Definitely, I will go back now and tell Betty what we are going to do, and I am sure Betty and the other females can work out the best path to use, and if necessary, move stones and small rocks to make steps for Penny. On the day you are coming up, all the goats will escort you up the side of the waterfall and tell Penny where to go, or if Penny needs a rock or two moving to make it easier for her to climb up, we will use our horns and feet to move them around. After all Penny can talk to us herself and tell us what she needs. We can make it fun and some of last year's babies are nearly fully grown now so they can lend a hand too as they are still with us. It will give them something to do to use their energy."

"That sounds like a great plan Bertie," laughed Izzy. "I will see you sometime tomorrow."

"Yes I will see you tomorrow," replied Bertie as he turned away from the waterfall and disappeared into the thicket of bushes and trees. Izzy took a few more moments to drink in the atmosphere and imprint the image of the staircase leading to the cave on her mind so she could describe everything to the fairies, elves, animals and Penny tonight at the meeting. As she stood on the steps there was suddenly a huge flash of white which lit up the sky and then a loud crash. Izzy jumped in fright and fell down the last two steps of the staircase, where Bertie had deposited her before heading off back to his wives, onto the ground.

"What on earth was that," wailed Izzy to no one in particular. Suddenly she realised that the sky had become very dark too.

"Oh no," exclaimed Izzy. "I know what this is, we are in for a thunderstorm."

Just then the first few fat raindrops hit the surface of the waterfall pool. Izzy scrambled to her feet but realised she was not going to have time to reach neither the cave nor Penny's garden before the deluge of rain descended so she frantically looked around for some other place to shelter while the storm raged. Suddenly she spied a stone with a tiny hole in it at the side of the step just above her head. The hole was so tiny she wasn't even sure if she could fit in it, and hoped fervently that it was not a sleeping fairy's home as she knew if it was already occupied there would be no room for her. She scrambled to her feet and poked her head inside the hole. Good, as far as she could see or hear there was no evidence of occupation. Just at that moment the expected deluge of water arrived and hit Izzy firmly on her bottom. With a shriek Izzy frantically scrambled into the hole. She had to fold her wings tightly to her body, and drawing her feet up to her chest, she was able to just squeeze into the hole. She realised that this was the reason it wasn't occupied by a fairy or elf as there wasn't enough room to lie down comfortably, so with heartfelt gratitude Izzy settled herself down the best she could to wait for the storm to pass. It was so dark that each bolt of lightening lit up the sky and produced a myriad of colours from the water cascading down from the waterfall and the sky. The rain was pelting down on the rocks sending huge splashes all around Izzy's tiny sheltering hole. The pool at the bottom of the waterfall began to quickly fill up as the waterfall cascaded down, gathering momentum as the rain continued to fall.

At each clap of thunder Izzy winced, as it resonated off the rocks around her, and the waterfall and pool made a natural amphitheatre for the spectacular storm as it crashed about overhead. Suddenly a torrent of water came cascading over the steps, that only a few minutes ago, Izzy had been gazing at to imprint on her mind in readiness for tonight's meeting. Izzy shrank back further into her hiding place to try to stop getting splashed by the raging water. She couldn't make herself much smaller and hoped that the opening was high enough up to remain above the water level, although to be honest she wasn't too sure about it.

As the thunder slowly receded away into the distance and the lightening bolts became less frequent the sky began to lighten and the sun returned. Izzy gasped at the scene in front of her. The rain drops, that although still falling but with less intensity, hung like jewels shimmering on a beautiful necklace in the rays of the sun. The rocks, plants and bushes around the waterfall sparkled after the rain wash they had just received and the deluge of water cascading down the steps slowed down to a mere trickle. The steps shone and sparkled and suddenly the air became alive with insects and then to Izzy's surprise fairies, elves and pixies emerged from every crevice, plant and stone to revel in the puddles, jumping, splashing and dancing amongst the rain drops and slide down the sun beams. Laughing Izzy emerged from her own hiding place and joined her subjects in their games.

At first they were in awe of this, their Fairy Queen, enjoying the newly washed air but once they realised she was enjoying it as much as them, they cast off their shyness and joined in with her. During a bout of vigorous splashing in a puddle with some of her young subjects she was treated to the spectacular sight of the birds and the remaining fairies and elves appearing from the direction of Penny's garden and the surrounding area until the waterfall, pool, rocks, plants and bushes were covered in the shimmering colours of her subjects. The bees emerged to begin to gather the last traces of pollen. The butterflies emerged and began stretching their wings to get them dried and warmed by the sun. The birds of the forest descended to the waterfall pool to bathe and splash in the water, the water voles began to collect grass and leaves to use to line their homes or repair any damage done by the raging water.

Izzy was soon flanked by her deputies Mercury, Sapphire, Topaz and Emerald while they all frolicked in the abating rainstorm. Soon all the rain had passed and the sun emerged properly to dry the rocks. Izzy and her deputies found a beautiful flat stone that they could lie out on and let the sun dry out their wings, and Izzy was able to recount all the adventures she had experienced during the day and tell them about all the animals she had met.

She outlined her ideas for the island to make accommodation for visiting fairies and elves and about the cave she had found behind the waterfall that would make an excellent banqueting hall or small intimate ballroom. The other fairies knew nothing about the cave but Mercury assured Izzy that she was sure there were plenty of fairies or elves who would be able to come up with suggestions on how to light it.

Obviously they knew about the staircase but had never followed it to see where it led. Again the deputies felt that lighting it would not be a problem and, like Izzy, that it would provide a spectacular, unusual feature for their kingdom. Her deputies felt that providing alternative accommodation for visitors would be welcomed by the other fairies and elves, so that they would not have to share their homes with fairies and elves from other kingdoms.

The thought of having the chance to line their homes with the goat hair got everyone very excited. It was felt that as soon as they had got their homes established they would get a working party together to collect the hair. They were sure it would be very easy to organise, especially if Penny and Izzy could introduce them to the goats, so they could access the paths that the goats used regularly. Izzy assured them that once the 'wool gathering party' had been formed she would personally introduce them to the goats and thought it would be possible for them to travel with the goats on a daily basis until enough wool had been gathered. Izzy was telling her deputies about riding on Bertie's head and how soft and warm the seat had been when one of her subjects approached.

"I am sorry Queen Izzy but I couldn't help overhearing your conversation about the goats. Are these the ones who come into the clearing during the winter?"

"Why yes that is Bertie and his wives," she answered. "Do you know them?"

"Yes a few of us know them real well and often bury ourselves, unbeknown to them, in their hair, especially on real cold days," answered the young elf. "I would be happy to head a party that would keep our kingdom supplied with wool from their coats. We have a pretty good idea of the paths they frequently use too, but there isn't much around at the moment."

"No there won't be," answered Izzy, "because they spend most of the time up on the side of the waterfall. In the early spring they have small babies who can't make the trip down but they have promised to meet Penny and me in the clearing in the next few days. If you come with us I can introduce you and then leave you to form your own working party. Does that sound okay to you and could you please remind me of your name? I know you introduced yourself last night but I have already forgotten it. I am so sorry?"

"No worries ma'am, I am Finn, and I would be honoured to take the role of ensuring we always have enough goat wool to keep our kingdom homes warm. What about the visitor accommodation, will that need lining too?"

"I imagine so Finn but I am hoping Penny can come up with some ideas how to provide that accommodation tonight. She said something this morning about hotels and holiday park before she left for work, but no one I have spoken to today has any idea what she was taking about. She said she would explain when she came back from work so until then I am no wiser."

"Well I will speak to the fairies and elves who I think will make a responsible initial team but we can always recruit more if we need them."

"That would be great Finn, you go ahead with that. I am having a kingdom meeting tonight in Penny's garden of all my kingdom subjects, well those that can get into the garden anyway, at sundown, so maybe after the meeting has finished you can come and introduce yourself to Penny and she can expand on this hotel, holiday home theme. That way we can all understand what might be needed," answered Izzy.

"Thank you ma'am I will do that," replied Finn. "Maybe my brother Fergal could be my deputy as he knows the goats too. That way you have two of us you can cascade information to."

"Thank you Finn. If you get Fergal to introduce himself too and bring him to our select committee meeting after the main meeting tonight. Now I need to identify a head of lighting. Any ideas girls or you Finn? Anyone want to offer any suggestions?" enquired Izzy.

Suddenly a tiny fairy fluttered on to the rock next to Izzy.

"Please ma'am, could I be considered for the role of head of lighting person?"

"Of course Mimi, you are the most obvious person. Why didn't we think about you when Izzy was telling us about needing lighting for the staircase and cave? After all you have already started to deal with the lighting around Penny's garden and this is just an extension of that. Izzy meet Mimi, she uses glow worms where she can but also catches raindrops and suspends them to get coloured lights as well. She is the best lighting person we know," explained Topaz. "You may need some assistants though now Mimi, as this Fairy Queen of ours has some very ambitious plans for our kingdom."

"Yes I am afraid you are all going to be working flat out from now on," laughed Izzy. "Sometimes I get a bit carried away so you deputies had better reign me in occasionally."

"Oh no, we are loving all your enthusiasm and plans," replied Mercury, "and I know all the fairies and elves feel the same. Last night after you left there was such a buzz amongst them and they all vowed to make Penny's Kingdom the best kingdom in the land. No, I was just pointing out to Mimi that she would need a team around her to keep on top of the work."

"That is okay Queen Izzy I have a couple of elves and fairies that I think I can train to help me look after all the lighting of our kingdom and we can always train more if we need more," explained Mimi.

"Right, so I know I have a lighting team and a 'wool gathering team'. I think I will call them our interior team, as they will be responsible for the interiors of the homes. Anything else anyone can think of?" asked Izzy.

"I think we might need someone to oversee the gathering of food especially for when we have visitors and possibly someone to keep our kingdom headquarters clean and tidy," observed Sapphire.

"Brilliant," exclaimed Izzy. "We can't expect the fairies and elves to look after our communal areas as well as their homes. It might have to be all hands on deck after a big party or ball and all of us will have to pitch in as there will a lot of mess after one of them, but otherwise we just need someone to keep an eye on the headquarters and make sure everything remains in good working order. And yes Sapphire, absolutely, we need someone to be in charge of ensuring there is enough food especially when we have visiting fairies and elves. Now anyone got any suggestions or shall we just bring it up at the meeting tonight?"

"I can't think of anyone at the moment for either of those jobs," replied Mercury, "but I will give it some thought before we meet tonight. I think it might be good to have all our heads of operations in place tonight so they can be introduced to our kingdom and then they can get on with their job of putting their teams together so we are ready to push ahead as the kingdom develops. It looks as if our queen has surpassed herself today getting to grips with her many subjects so it is up to us now to help her realise her dream of a super fairy kingdom. What about meeting up for a few minutes before you open the meeting Izzy so we can inform you who we have come up with to head our ground and catering staff?"

"That sounds like a good plan, actually why don't we meet earlier, before my subjects start to assemble, that way I can meet my new operational heads that I haven't met before and get to know Finn, Fergal and Mimi better. Can you think of a second in command that you can rely on Mimi to work alongside you?" enquired Izzy.

"Yes I think my best friend Mo would make an excellent deputy for me. She often helps me with any big jobs when I need someone to hold something or problems like that. She might not, at this point, be able to actually deputise for me but I can soon train her as she appears interested in everything I do. There hasn't been, previously, enough to keep me busy, never mind a deputy, but it sounds as though the 'lighting team' could be kept rather busy if we are maintaining a ballroom, outside staircase, visiting fairy accommodation as well as resident fairy homes and headquarters. If we add four fairy balls a year, including a Winter National Ball, then I can see I will not only need a deputy or two but an expanding team of fairies and elves to follow our plans and get the work done. I will be honoured to head your 'lighting team' Queen Izzy and even the small plans I have overheard appear to be ambitious and fun," observed Mimi.

"Thank you Mimi, I look forward to working with you and taking advice from you as to the feasibility of my plans. Please come along this evening and bring Mo, your intended deputy, to officially meet Penny, and I will do my best to outline my immediate requirements and give you an overall view of where we might be heading, although please don't take them as set in concrete. As we evolve we might head off in a different direction knowing me," laughed Izzy.

"Don't worry Queen Izzy I can assure you that we will carry out your wishes as best as we can. If you do come up with something that I feel is impossible I will happily offer you a alternative but certainly what I have heard there is nothing that can't be done. The visitor accommodation may need more thought once we know exactly what it might entail," answered Mimi.

"Well to be honest Mimi until Penny explains to me what hotels and holiday homes are, that she briefly mentioned this morning, I am as much in the dark as you. Mercury, do you think it would be a good idea to meet in Penny's cottage, before the meeting, with just my deputies and our operation heads and their deputies? Have we enough responsible fairies and elves to oversee the gathering of those subjects who are likely to be affected by our plans Mercury? I intend to have a larger meeting of all my subjects in the clearing which will include the deer, goats, squirrels, rabbits and foxes that I have met today and any other animals that I haven't met but tonight I felt that the birds, hedgehogs, mice, that as yet I haven't met, water voles and all you fairies, elves and pixies who are involved in the fairy kingdom headquarters need to be briefed about our plans. Those who reside deeper in the forest are not likely to be directly affected by our activities," commented Izzy.

"Of course Queen Izzy that sounds like a good plan if you think Penny won't mind having her cottage invaded by a swarm of fairies and elves! It might be a good idea to have a team of fairies and elves who oversee the advertising and organisation of these full meetings as we expand our operations but in the meantime I can certainly round up enough to start us off tonight. Actually it might be a good idea to use the 'ground staff' to include meeting duties to their role and I have just this minute thought of a couple of fairies and elves that would be excellent at heading that team. Emerald, how about Anna, Andy and maybe Fee to head the ground staff. Anna is excellent at gardening and landscape work, which might be useful, especially around the visitor accommodation and as Andy is her twin he tunes into her plans and can interpret what she is trying to do. Fee is so clever at creating things from wood and metal and mending things that get broken I am sure he will prove invaluable," enquired Mercury.

"Why yes of course that trio will make excellent heads of the ground staff. I am sure all three will be able to put a team together to maintain all the areas and keep everything looking smart and well cared for. That just leaves us with the question of someone who can head the catering team. Come on Topaz and Sapphire, I am sure somewhere we must have a fairy or elf who has the knowledge and creative skills to head a team of catering staff. It needs someone who can work closely with Finn and his team to gather berries and nuts when they are out 'wool gathering' and Anna and Andy who might have to design areas that we can grow things in to provide a variation to everyone's diet. I know normally fairies and elves gather their own provisions but I have a feeling that all the fairies and elves of our kingdom will be kept busy ensuring our kingdom runs smoothly," instructed Emerald.

"I am sorry Emerald but I can't think of a single fairy or elf that could be left in charge of the catering," explained Sapphire. "How about you Topaz?"

"No I can't either, how about the rest of you newly appointed heads, Finn or Mimi?" asked Topaz.

Finn stepped forward hesitantly.

"I know you don't know Gina and Bella very well yet, as they have only just joined us, but they have been giving us some great tips to vary our diets of berries and nuts. For example they suggested we go further afield and gather some oats and barley which we can grid down and add different berries to and also different plants we can use so I think they might make excellent heads of catering. I think they might prefer to lead jointly as they seem to bounce ideas of each other but I don't know."

"Well done Finn," exclaimed Topaz and Sapphire in unison. "We did overhear them giving tips and suggestions the other day, but as you mentioned, because they haven't been with us very long we didn't immediately think about them to head this team. Where are they today I don't think I have seen them?"

"They have taken a few of our younger fairies and elves to forage in the forest and see what is growing that we can use so they have, unbeknown to them, started to put a team together. Fergal and I will go with them next time so we can explore the forest and its array of produce through fresh eyes," answered Finn.

"Perfect, so Izzy between us all, we have identified you your heads of operations. You have Finn and Fergal heading your 'interior' team, Mimi and Mo your lighting, team, Anna, Andy and Fee who are your ground staff leaders and finally Gina and Bella who will head your catering team. Does that sound okay?" asked Mercury.

"It is more than okay, it is awesome," exclaimed Izzy. "Thank you team, now we need to make sure all the heads know to come to Penny's cottage, before we join the rest of the members of the kingdom in the garden to introduce the leaders of each team and outline the plans for the expansion of the headquarters and the kingdom as a whole. How do we ensure that everyone knows about this, as I haven't given any of you much time to round up the heads and let them know about the first meeting? We need to give ourselves plenty of time to discuss the plans in detail especially the new venture of providing visitor accommodation before we head out to the main meeting," asked Izzy.

"I will go and brief Fergal now and then if you want I can catch up with Gina and Bella when they get back," suggested Finn.

"Well if you just brief Fergal and get him up to speed on your roles as well as begin putting a team together, I will ensure personally, that I meet up with Gina and Bella and outline their duties. Emerald how about you find the 'ground staff' heads and brief them? Topaz and Sapphire, can you two take responsibility for informing the other fairies, elves and the birds that live in and around Penny's garden about the meeting? Mimi if you brief Mo and begin putting your team together then I think we might manage between us to round everyone up. Does that help you Izzy?" asked Mercury.

"Absolutely as I want to go and visit the mice and hedgehogs now so I can issue their invitations to the meeting. I didn't mention the meeting to the water voles this morning, as when I spoke to them I hadn't thought about it. Technically they live outside the garden but I am sure the area where they live will be impacted by our plans, so I guess I had better include a visit to them too," answered Izzy.

"I will visit the water voles and extend your invitation if you want Queen Izzy, as I am living over there at the moment. Fergal lives close by too so if you want some of your management team to live near the visitor accommodation block then we would be honoured to oblige," suggested Finn.

"Yes Finn that is an excellent idea if you are happy living over there. We need to think about a proper home for you that you can line, so you stay cosy and warm in the winter though. The rest of our subjects will be living in Penny's garden with old pots, pans, kettles and things to use as homes but out there near the island we need to find something that blends in so even if another human strays into the area they won't notice your home. Any suggestions at this point?" asked Izzy.

"Well actually, yes I have Queen Izzy. There is a small tree stump just over the stream close to the island. It needs work on it to enlarge some holes around the base but if we can do that, then Fergal and I will happily line it and make it comfortable," offered Finn.

"How about asking the ground staff team to help you Finn," suggested Izzy.

"Check with the water voles that the area doesn't flood," piped up Emerald. "You need to make sure that your home is not going to flood Finn, if it is near the stream. Remember, you are building yourself a forever home."

"Oh I hadn't thought about that," mused Finn. "I had maybe better have another think."

"If you want to live in your tree stump and it is tall enough why not make your home higher up. You will need to make holes higher up but I am sure something can be worked out," suggested Sapphire.

"Why not get the woodpeckers, who live in the forest, to bore you new holes higher up?" Topaz suggested shyly.

"Excellent Topaz," replied Izzy. "You see how already the team are working together. I suggest you and Fergal go and talk to the water voles and inspect your tree stump to see how it can be used to make you a home. Do you know the woodpeckers Topaz?"

"Yes all the birds are my close friends so if Sapphire is happy I will go and visit all the birds who live in and around Penny's garden. Maybe in time Penny can make homes for the birds to live in. The robins, who live here all winter, would especially appreciate some warm homes for the winter," Topaz answered. "I will go now to issue the invitations if you want so I can get back in time for the first meeting as I might have to go into the forest to find them all. Shall I send the woodpeckers to meet you and Fergal near the island while I am on my travels?"

"That would be brilliant Topaz I will go and find Fergal now. I wonder if the tree stump would provide homes for our team as we won't need many of us to gather wool and provisions," answered Finn. "I imagine we will probably only need about four or five workers, in addition to Fergal and me, maybe not even that many at first, until we start to have more visitors."

"I don't think any of you will need large numbers in your teams at first Finn, but that might change with such dynamic and forward looking queen," laughed Mercury. "Now I will go and look for Gina and Bella and welcome them properly to our kingdom and brief them on their suggested duties. Emerald off you go and brief Anna, Andy and Fee and if you go and sort out the rest of the elves and fairies Sapphire, I think we have covered it all. You go and talk to the hedgehogs and mice Izzy and then you had better prepare Penny for the invasion of fairies and elves that will be occurring soon."

"Yes thank you girls you have been a great help already and I know you will continue to be so as we grow and expand our kingdom. Topaz if you hear of anything the birds want or need make sure you tell either me or Penny and the same goes for you others."

"What about giving us all areas of responsibilities Izzy?" asked Mercury.

"Good idea. Topaz you work with the birds, Sapphire with the fairies and elves, Emerald with the 'ground staff' and Mercury you can work with the catering team. I will liaise with Penny to make sure the animals are catered for and we will get some containers placed around the garden to use as homes for the fairies and elves. What about you four, I know where you were sleeping this morning but that is not going to afford you much protection in winter?" asked Izzy.

"Well we wondered if we could use Penny's summer house to live in now we know she has the gift of seeing and talking to us. We had a quick look last night and there is a space between the roof and the walls that we can squeeze through and maybe if we talk to Penny she can suggest somewhere inside that we can each call our home. That way all our subjects know where to find us, sorry we mean your subjects Izzy, if they have any problems," replied Mercury.

"Excellent idea, very fitting for my deputies to live in the summer house as I will continue to live in the cottage with Penny, Trixie and Dixie. Penny is making me my own door to come and go from the cottage and maybe she can do something similar in the summer house, so she can block all the holes up which will make it much warmer for winter."

"Wow that would be wonderful Izzy if she could. Maybe she could put a door knocker on the door so the fairies and elves could knock on the door if they needed us."

"I am sure she will be able to come up with something. We can ask her tonight, so she can be giving it some thought," laughed Izzy. "Now I am going back to the garden to fulfil my duties and I suggest you all do the same. Then come and join Penny, me and the animals when you have finished organising everyone. Goodbye until we meet later."

Each fairy and elf left the rock that they had all been assembled on to attend to their allocated tasks calling goodbye to Izzy as they left, until only Izzy was left. With a final lingering glance at the beauty of the waterfall Izzy also unfolded her wings and flew off in the direction of Penny's garden feeling well satisfied with her day's work.

An Unexpected Visitor

Izzy landed in the garden near to the summer house and popped underneath it to see if she could find out if the hedgehog had given birth yet and to let them all know about the meeting tonight. She noticed that the lone male had shuffled his way over to be closer to Hetty and her babies and all were tucked up close together. The expectant mother was almost buried in the nest that she had been finishing off when Izzy had left her this morning. Izzy tiptoed across to the nest reluctant to disturb her but a sleepy voice piped up.

"Is that you Izzy? Come and meet my new babies."

"Yes it is me, I have had such a busy day it has taken me until now to get back to the garden. I am so pleased you have had them all okay. How many have you had?" replied Izzy.

"I have had four babies Izzy. You won't be able to see them as they are all snuggled in the nest and will be for quite a few days because they are born bare and blind so could easily catch cold. They won't venture out for quite a few weeks but I wanted you to know how many had been born so you can get Penny working on names for all her hedgehog family. Hetty's babies will be soon coming out on foraging trips with their mum, especially as they are quite safe in Penny's garden, and I will encourage mine to come out early too. So Izzy tell me what you have been doing all day," instructed the hedgehog.

"Well I have spent the day exploring the waterfall and the vicinity around it. I met some deer who migrate down into the forest in the autumn, wild goats, foxes, squirrels and rabbits. I almost got washed away during a massive thunderstorm but then had great fun playing in the sun with my subjects afterwards. I met the water voles and lots of different birds. My deputies and me have appointed heads to manage different sections of the kingdom and we are having a meeting with Penny tonight, although as yet she is unaware of it, in her cottage before the general meeting of all my subjects including you animals that may, or should I say, will be affected by the growth of the kingdom. I am aware you won't make the meeting tonight but I hope the rest will be able to come and then they can fill you in on all our plans or I can tomorrow."

"Wow Izzy, you have been busy. I am sorry I can't get tonight but I will look forward to hearing all about it later," laughed the hedgehog. "It sounds as though you are going to keep your deputies and subjects busy then."

"Yes everyone will be having to work flat out, but I will make sure they all have time to play and have fun too," answered Izzy. "I am just going to visit the mice under the patio to tell them about the meeting tonight and then go and wait in the house for Penny to come home. Do you think it will be alright to wake Hetty and the others to tell them about the meeting?"

"Of course it will be fine," answered the hedgehog.

"I am awake already Izzy and have been listening to your news," murmured Hetty "My babies will be able to come out with me soon but maybe not tonight, if there are going to be a lot of birds and people about. I wouldn't want anything to happen to them."

"I am sure they will be safe, the only animals coming tonight are you hedgehogs, the mice and possibly the water voles and the birds are only those who live in or close to the garden. Obviously Penny, me, my deputies and all the fairies and elves that are part of the kingdom but they will always be around."

"Oh in that case they may be okay then. I was worried we were going to have deer, wild goats, foxes and all the other animals you mentioned," replied Hetty.

"No," giggled Izzy. "There isn't enough room in the garden for goats, deer and the rest of the forest animals. I will hold a full kingdom meeting for everyone eventually in the clearing but this meeting is merely to outline the plans for the immediate development of the kingdom headquarters which will obviously impact on you to a certain degree. I am hoping Penny can shed some light on how we can accommodate our proposed visitors too. I intend to introduce the heads of the different operations to both you, the animals, and the fairies and elves. It shouldn't be a long meeting tonight as I, or rather we, haven't got any detail plans formulated only vague ideas and that goes for the summer ball too. Sometime over the next week or two we will have a further meeting to keep you abreast of our plans."

"Right well, apart from our new mum, you can count on us hedgehogs to be there to support you. What time is the meeting?" asked Hetty.

"At sundown Hetty," replied Izzy.

"Oh perfect just when we would be coming out to forage for food. Okay Izzy we will see you later. Where are you going now did you say?"

"I am just going to visit the mice who live under Penny's patio to invite them to the meeting and see how many are actually there Hetty."

"Well there always seems to be several scurrying back and forth but there might not be a great many. It may be the same ones we keep seeing over and over again," laughed Hetty. "They all look alike to me but I guess they may say the same about us."

"Oh tell me about it. I have spent the entire day trying to identify who was who in the deer family, and then again with the wild goats. I will at some point have to try to identify you hedgehogs but it is too cramped and dark at the moment. Also my head is mashed trying to work out the other animals. I am afraid it will be the same as I said to the rabbits I will work you all out eventually and the mice will be told the same. I just want to make myself known to them and explain who Penny is, and then invite them to the meeting, anything else can keep for another day. Goodbye for now Hetty I will see you later."

"Goodbye Izzy see you later."

With a wave of her hand Izzy slipped out from under the summer house and made her way across the garden to the patio. Here she saw the step and the small hole to one side. Izzy slipped easily inside, as the hole was not half as tiny as the one she had sheltered in earlier, and once her eyes had adjusted to the darkness she saw that there were several distinct areas located under there. At first Izzy thought that the areas were probably where different functions of life were attended to, but then realised that each large area was sub divided into smaller areas, and that in each sub division you had what was clearly a sleeping area and feeding area. These sub divisions were situated round the outside of a large circle and in this communal circle there was a number of mice of all ages lounging about. Suddenly a couple of mice spotted Izzy hovering in the doorway.

"Hello fairy, is it possible you are our queen? We heard about you from the other fairies last night as we collected our food and cleaned out our homes."

"Why yes I am Izzy, or maybe I should get used to introducing myself as Queen Izzy. I have popped in to introduce myself and say welcome to my kingdom. It is no use trying to introduce yourselves today, as I have met so many different animals and tried to get my head around their names. I really can't take any more in but please be assured that I will, in time, get to know you all better. How many of you live here, because the hedgehogs seemed unsure if there was lots of you, or just a few that they kept seeing over and over again? While I remember I am having a meeting in the garden tonight at sundown to outline our plans for the kingdom headquarters that we are developing here in Penny's garden. The other fairies and elves had begun work on it but were unsure if Penny would be happy to let them continue. Penny is one of those special people who can see and talk to fairies and elves but she can also hear and talk to animals too so she was delighted to have her garden become the kingdom headquarters," explained Izzy.

"Yes the fairies were so pleased and excited last night to tell us all about Penny and you, and how you are encouraging them to organise a Winter National Fairy Ball. Obviously if we can help in any way don't hesitate to ask. We have six families of mice here. Each family have their own space where they eat and sleep and then this communal space is used by everyone. In total there are twenty of us, all ages living here so we wouldn't expect you to remember us all, but you are welcome to visit any time you want. I am Arthur and I guess you would say I am the chief. I have three wives, several offspring and we also have relatives of my wives. These two handsome young boys are my sons, who will soon be leaving us to develop their own families. Most of the adult mice will be happy to attend the meeting but we have a new mum, who certainly can't leave the nest and her babies, and one of my wives is feeling a bit off colour so she will probably stay here and mind the younger members of the family."

"Oh another new mum. One of the hedgehogs just gave birth today so she won't be coming to the meeting either. I will be very pleased to see however many of you who can come, and I will be introducing Penny to you all too. I am so pleased to meet you Arthur, and look forward to visiting you for longer another day, but in the meantime I must go into the house and wait for Penny to come home as I am not too sure when that will be."

"I think Penny may have already come home as Trixie was playing in the garden a few minutes ago and then went hurtling into the house. That usually signifies that she has heard Penny's car," explained Arthur.

"Oh my goodness is that so, then I had better make haste and prepare Penny for the fact that very shortly her cottage is going to be swarming with fairies and elves as we are having a small meeting first with my deputies and operation heads that have been appointed today, before the full meeting of all my subjects in the garden."

"In that case I think you had better go Queen Izzy," laughed Arthur. "We will see you later, bye."

"Bye," replied Izzy as she left the mice.

Once she had readjusted to the light from the setting

sun she hopped up on to the patio and popped through her own little door into the kitchen. She flew up on to the worktop where Penny was preparing Dixie's food and suddenly stopped dead in her tracks. Not only was Penny there, but another human. Izzy was so flustered she wasn't sure what to do. Did she find something to hide behind, slip off the working top and slink back out into the garden or just stand her ground? Whilst she was making up her mind Dixie spied her and gently scooped her up.

"Oh there you are Izzy I wondered where you might be. Izzy this is Danny and it is okay he believes in fairies and elves but hasn't had the pleasure of meeting any real ones so I invited him over to meet you," explained Penny. "As usual Danny was picking up my fairy ornaments on my windowsill and peering closely at each one in turn. I asked him why he was examining them more closely than usual, and he confessed he had overheard the conversation between me and the control tower yesterday and wondered if he had heard me correctly that I had a fairy with me. I decided that I would tell him all about you, how we met, what happened after we got home last night, that you had been made the fairy queen and that the kingdom headquarters were going to be in my garden. The further into the story I got, the more engrossed he became, so I thought the best way to let him meet you was to invite him over for tea as I wasn't sure when you might have time to go into work with me. I did wonder if we might take another stroll to the waterfall again tonight to see if we might manage to see some of the others. Please say if you don't think we should."

"Well," began Izzy.

Just at that moment fairies and elves began tumbling through Izzy's little door. Dixie immediately left Izzy and jumped down to greet her friends. Penny looked to see why Dixie had got down and was amazed to witness a swarm of fairies and elves pouring into her kitchen

"What on earth is going on Izzy?" exclaimed Penny.

Danny's eyes were like saucers as he fumbled towards

a chair.

"Well I was trying to tell you Penny, that I had invited my deputies and heads of departments to come to this early meeting, so they could meet you and we could all get a better idea about these hotels and things you mentioned before you went to work this morning. Once the sun goes down we have a full kingdom headquarters meeting in the garden planned. I never expected you to bring Danny home with you, but since he is here and he wanted to meet some fairies and elves, he may as well join both meetings.

"Oh my goodness Danny I am so sorry to throw you in at the deep end. Izzy never does things by half so I should have been prepared for something like this," laughed Penny.

"Please don't be sorry Penny I think I must have died and gone to heaven. Please will you all stay still so I can count you all," breathed Danny.

"I can do better than that I will introduce you personally to those I know. I have to confess there are some who I know should be here, but that I didn't meet this afternoon when we were discussing who was going to be involved in which department," confessed Izzy.

"What on earth are you talking about Izzy? What departments? What have you been up to whilst I have been at work?" asked Penny.

"Well now that is rather a long story. Come on, let me introduce you both to everyone then while you sort some tea out for you and Danny I, or rather we, will tell you the full story of exactly what I have been up to all day. Oh by the way you have several hedgehogs to name when you can get your head together," laughed Izzy.

"Well Izzy you continue to surprise me. I can see my life is never going to be mundane and boring with you around. How about it Danny, are you game for this or do you want to run out of the door now and never come back?"

"No way am I leaving," exclaimed Danny. "There is no way you are keeping me away from this crazy house now.

I was on tenterhooks wondering if Izzy would actually let me meet her and suddenly here I am surrounded by a host of fairies and elves and, if I have understood this right, before the night is finished will have met several more."

"Great," laughed Izzy, "welcome to the world of Penny's Kingdom. Right here goes Danny. Meet Mercury, Emerald, Sapphire and Topaz they are my deputies but they are also going to manage a department too but more of that later."

"Well that bit is easy as I can identify you all by the colour of your dress as your name reflects the colour of it."

"What are you talking about Danny? How does the colour of the dresses my deputies are wearing reflect their name?" asked Izzy.

"I can answer that Izzy," answered Penny. "I didn't realise last night, because it was almost dark, but us humans have precious stones that are different colours so Emerald is green, Sapphire blue and Topaz is yellow. Mercury is a beautiful liquid which is mainly a silvery grey colour with flashes of other colours running through it just like your dress Mercury."

"Well I never," exclaimed Izzy. "What kind of dress is this one of mine then Penny?"

"Yours is a bright diamond white with threads of gold and silver shooting through it, very fitting for a queen as diamond, gold and silver are more precious than the other gem stones but please continue introducing me and Danny to the rest of the fairies and elves," instructed Penny.

"Well actually I will now hand over to Mercury to introduce the rest of them as I don't know them all personally," laughed Izzy. "I trusted my deputies to identify and recruit them after we parted company this afternoon. Over to you Mercury."

"Hello Danny, pleased to meet you. Penny and Danny meet Finn and Fergal who are going to head our interior team. Finn and Fergal will be in charge of collecting wool off the bushes and branches from the wild goats to line all our resident homes, collecting berries and plants for the catering staff to use, collecting other plants and seeds to either use directly or plant to grow our own supply and anything else they think can be of use to furnish our homes or communal spaces."

Two elves stepped forward both dressed identically in green apart from one had a pointed hat and the other a flat cap. The one with the pointed hat introduced himself as Finn and then the one with the flat cap shyly introduced himself as Fergal.

"Finn and Fergal are close friends with the wild goats so can keep us supplied with plenty of wool to keep all our homes and the visitor accommodation warm and cosy," explained Izzy.

"Hang on a minute, what visitor accommodation and where in heavens name do the wild goats live?" asked Penny.

"Ah well the visitor accommodation is yet to be properly discussed between us all, but I have found a perfect little island that I hope we can develop to provide accommodation for visiting fairies and elves. You mentioned this morning about hotels and holiday homes which neither I, nor anyone I have spoken to today, have a remote idea what they would look like but you said you would show me a picture tonight," answered Izzy.

"So I did," replied Penny.

"I can help here," piped up Danny, "as I have a holiday home on a camp site just up the road in a forest and there are a few trees that have the appearance of fairy hotels. I don't know if that is what they are or if anyone stays there but if you, Izzy, go with Penny and me, maybe even some of you others, we could investigate."

Izzy clapped her hands in delight.

"Perfect Danny we will discuss that a bit later, in the meantime Mercury carry on please."

"This is Mimi and Mo, they will be heading our lighting team. We will need the whole of the kingdom headquarters lighting, visitor accommodation but Izzy also discovered a tiny cave behind the waterfall that is accessed by a wonderful staircase so both of these will require lighting. Izzy suggested using the cave for a banqueting hall or small intimate ballroom for when we have visiting dignitaries."

Two fairies stepped forward.

"I am Mimi and this is my friend Mo, Penny and Danny. We will both be pleased to serve our wonderful Queen Izzy. If you have any suggestions don't hesitate to give us a shout."

"Pleased to meet you Mimi and Mo," acknowledged Penny and Danny.

"Yes Mo pleased to make your acquaintance as I didn't meet you this afternoon. Do you think you will be happy working alongside Mimi on all our lighting needs?" asked Izzy.

"Oh definitely, Queen Izzy, I have always enjoyed helping Mimi when I could but never thought I would get the chance to work with her every day. She will also make an excellent teacher. I just hope I can help Mimi to deliver what you all need"

"I am sure you will do fine Mo. Okay Mercury, the rest of the team are all strangers to me so go ahead and introduce them to Penny, Danny and me."

"This is Gina and Bella who will be heading your catering team Izzy. Gina was telling me earlier that we have an extensive array of wild berries and nut trees in the forest, and if you head on to the moorland area, there are several more different species of berries. Although, at the moment, there are not many berries or nuts available but they will prepare some larders to store them when they are ripe in the autumn so we can have a varied diet throughout the winter. They say there is evidence of wild strawberries and raspberries growing as well as brambles. They have found some grain fields that can be ground to add to berries and a field of oilseed rape which if you crush the flowers you can get oil from to use as dressings. They are going to work closely with Finn and Fergal's team to gather the harvest in and Anna to plant seeds to grow our own. Anna and Andy will identify a patch of good soil to use for planting provisions for the year. Gina and Bella, meet your queen properly tonight. I know you met her last night but she met so many of you she wasn't able to get to know you properly. It was the same for Penny and now we have a new human recruit in Danny."

Two fairies detached themselves from the group who were waiting to be introduced. Both gave a small curtsey to Izzy then to Penny and lastly to Danny.

"Pleased to meet you Queen Izzy, Penny and Danny. I am Gina and this is my sister Bella."

"We are pleased to meet you too Gina and Bella. I am afraid I have no idea about gathering or storing food because my family never left our garden and we just ate what was available. Listening to what Mercury has just been telling me I can see my subjects are going to be well fed under your directions. If you need anything further just ask. Penny might be a better source of inspiration than me," said Izzy.

"I can probably help with some of this," offered Danny. "I have an extensive fruit and vegetable plot at home and I would be willing to give you a tour if you want."

"Excellent idea Danny, thank you so much," exclaimed Izzy.

"Yes thank you Danny. We have had a quick look around Penny's garden but there is only flowers which are excellent because that means we will have many bees visiting the garden so we will get a constant supply of nectar to use as a sweetener. If you have a selection of fruit bushes then we can use them until we get our own supply sorted," answered Gina.

"Now you last three must be my ground staff. Would you like to introduce yourselves please?" asked Izzy.

"Hello Queen Izzy I am Anna. I will take on the responsibility of designing all our outside spaces and this is Andy who does a lot of the heavy digging and erecting of items. He is looking forward to working closely with Gina and Bella because, like Danny, his passion is soft fruit trees and bushes and planting grasses and grains to provide seeds. The last member of our trio is Fee who is excellent at designing and making things out of wood or metal. He especially loves to get things that other people have thrown away and fashion them into something useful. Penny, I will need to work closely with you so that I don't spoil your garden but so we can provide for the kingdom."

"Oh I wouldn't worry about that," laughed Penny. "There is no set pattern to my garden. Flowers jostle each other constantly and I am sure if you look deeply you might find evidence of barley or wheat growing that the birds have dropped. Please feel free to develop my garden into a productive kingdom headquarters. I did say to Izzy that I was sure I had a loft full of old pots, pans, kettles maybe even the odd teapot that I was happy to place around the garden to make homes for fairies, elves and even birds if they wanted them but apart from that my garden is just a wilderness."

"Well I am sure between us we can develop your garden so that it still looks pretty, will entice bees and butterflies and provide cover for all the fairies and elves if they want to hide. If you look out the containers I will design the garden around them although I think you humans might have to place them for us," laughed Anna. "Once everything is in place we will let Fee loose on developing other interesting bits and pieces. I would be interested in joining you on your proposed visit to the campsite and your garden Danny, as I might pick up some useful tips."

"You would be most welcome to join us Anna. Well to be honest you fairies and elves aren't going to take up much space so if you all wanted a trip out I am sure we can sort something out," assured Danny. "Meanwhile I would be pleased to welcome you too Andy to my garden which is completely different to Penny's, hardly a flower in sight."

"Well thank you Mercury for introducing us to the full team. Now Penny you had better get yourself and Danny some tea ready while we, the fairies and elves, fill you in about all we have learnt and done today. Have you any of that fruit, seed and nut mixture you gave me last night for tea as it was scrumptious?" asked Izzy.

"Well yes I got some more today, but I also found some soft fruits that you can have. Danny are you happy with pizza and salad as I haven't time to do anything else now this little imp has organised a meeting at such short notice without warning me?" answered Penny.

"Yes pizza and salad sounds fine Penny. If you give me the salad ingredients and a bowl I will do that part for us. You get the pizza ready and started to cook then we can sort some food out for our unexpected guests. I wasn't aware when I left home this morning that by this evening I would be sharing a meal with not one fairy but with fourteen little people. Pinch me Penny I think I must be dreaming!" laughed Danny.

"Yes I know how you feel, I was the same yesterday. Izzy has only been with me one day and she has already presented me with a myriad of challenges and by the sounds of it there will be many more to come. My biggest challenge right at this minute is trying to work out how to make this fruit into small enough bits so the fairies and elves can pick it up to eat. I remember now from last night how Izzy could only just manage the fruit, nut and seed mix by picking out one piece at a time. The raspberries, blackberries and blueberries I bought today are going to be far too big. I managed to find a thimble for Izzy to eat from last night but I certainly haven't fourteen thimbles! I wonder what I can find in the cupboard to use as a platter for the little people. Izzy, will it be okay if I put your food on the smallest dish I can find, and you all help yourselves? At the moment I haven't anything for you all to sit on but I will give it some thought for another time. Are you planning on regularly holding meetings here in my cottage?" asked Penny.

"I don't know, to be honest Penny, if the fairies and elves will be happy to have the food on one big plate to help themselves," answered Izzy. "I have never hosted neither a party nor a meeting. Mercury will everyone be happy with Penny's suggestion?"

"Of course we will," replied Mercury. "That is how we always eat when we eat as a group."

Finn stepped forward.

"Please Penny if you don't mind, could we bring you a temporary table into the cottage to use as and when we need it whilst you look for something better? I know of a piece of driftwood that would do as a temporary measure. Without a team of workers though, I am not sure if we can get it from the garden into the house. We certainly can't get it through the hole we all came through earlier."

"Could I help Finn," asked Danny. "If you show me the piece of wood I can pick it up and bring it into the house for you. Here pop onto my hand and we will go through the door. Is that alright with you Penny?"

"Yes of course, off you both go and bring me my new fairy table. If you find something nice and interesting it can stay on our big table forever. I would need to make some seats for it ready for next time but I would be honoured to have you all for tea whenever you want to come then."

Bella flew on to Penny's hand.

"Gina and I can prepare the fruit for the party for you Penny if you want, as we are planning on getting fruit from the forest for the kingdom when it is ready. How on earth could you get berries as early in the year as this?"

"Now are you Gina or Bella? I know it is one of you because you are wearing dresses that have black and white checks on but you both look the same," questioned Penny. "I could get the berries from the supermarket as they can get them all the year round as they come from another country. You are definitely welcome to prepare the fruit ready for your banquet too. Please take over and tell me if I can help at all."

"I am Bella, I have black hair that is how you can tell us apart Penny. Gina has white hair."

"Oh so you do," Penny exclaimed.

"Well done Penny, I was wondering how to tell Gina and Bella apart too. I never thought to look at their hair," mused Izzy.

"Show me the fruit you have got please Penny so I can see what tools I will need," instructed Bella.

Just then Gina fluttered up on to the worktop to help her sister with the food preparation.

"If you want we are happy to prepare all the food," offered Gina. "We need some plates and cups though too."

"The leaves from the jasmine plant just outside the door will make perfect plates," observed Anna from her place perched on the wind chime near the open window. "I can see that you had snowdrops in winter, and now the bluebells are out they will make excellent fairy showers Penny. We just need to ensure we have other flowers in the garden that will take over when the bluebells die. I will have to give it some thought."

"I can prepare a varnish to coat the leaves so they don't dry out," piped up Andy. "The plates can then stay in Penny's cottage for us whenever we want to have a meeting."

Just then Danny emerged from the garden holding a large piece of driftwood in one hand and several flat stones in the other. Finn was perched on the piece of wood.

"Gosh," shrieked Izzy, "that is a huge table for us."

Fee flew over to examine it in detail.

"Great," he said, "this is so big I can do lots of carving on it and it will still be large enough for us to eat off, spread plans out on it or whatever we need to use it for. Penny are you happy to let me work on this to make it pretty so it can stay on your table all the time?"

"Of course I am Fee, it is Fee isn't it? I can tell you by your paint splattered brown jumper," laughed Penny.

Fee looked down at his jumper and shrugged his shoulders.

"Yes Penny, I am Fee, and I am afraid all my clothes have paint splattered on. What else have you got there

Danny? Oh some lovely flat stones, these will make wonderful seats for round the table. I can paint them in lots of bright colours to match Penny's kitchen."

Mo stepped forward from where she had been observing Penny preparing the food for her and Danny.

"I have some spare material that would make a wonderful tablecloth that we can decorate with petals from the flowers if you want Penny?" she said.

"And I can put some twinkling light into it so it shimmers," offered Mimi.

"Oh my goodness you are all brilliant. I love the ideas you are all developing. You mean I can have a real fairy table and seats here in my kitchen. Dixie you had better be careful if you jump on the table and not knock anything off," instructed Penny.

"Oh I don't think neither Dixie nor Trixie will harm anything belonging to us fairies, they never do in the garden," observed Mercury "Okay so we have a table, seating, tablecloth and plates so all we need now is cups or wine goblets. Anyone got any suggestions team?"

"Well I can't do anything for tonight but by tomorrow I can have made something or what about using flowers as cups?" asked Fee. "Surely among all Penny's flowers there must be something that we can use as cups."

"I noticed a clump of white flowers with tiny cup like flowers peeping out from under a bush as we flew across the garden tonight. If we use them tonight can you use the same varnish as you are going to use on the plates Andy?" asked Fergal.

"Of course I can," answered Andy. "Can you show me and Anna where this plant is Fergal, as we may need to plant more to get flowers to use in the visitor accommodation and when we are holding the balls during the year."

"Yes come on Andy, I will show you which I mean. We will collect some jasmine leaves on our way back too. Can we borrow this basket please Penny as we don't want to crush the flowers?" asked Fergal.

"What basket, oh my goodness that was part of a Christmas decoration that Dixie decided to trash last year. I hadn't realised that it was still in the house. I wonder where it has been all these months?" mused Penny.

"Well Dixie has just brought it from somewhere in her month and laid it at my feet," laughed Fergal. "So I guess this is her way of helping us. Come on then let us go and find our cups and plates."

"I will come with you too," answered Anna, "so I can see what plant you are using, then I can save some seeds from it or get Penny to help me move it so it has more room to expand. I think I know which you mean but I will come and check."

"I will go and get my tablecloth for you," Mo decided.

"And we need our fruit knives to prise the seeds off. If we are having a tablecloth can you find me a large leaf that we can use as a platter? It will also need varnishing Andy if you find anything."

"That is okay Gina I can varnish everything that needs varnishing," replied Andy.

"If I draw up my proposed designs before I begin carving Penny can you can tell me if you want anything changing?" asked Fee.

"I am sure whatever you come up with Fee will be wonderful but it would be nice to see the proposed design," replied Penny.

"Okay Penny I will do. Now elves and fairies let us go and find everything we need. See you in a few minutes Penny, Danny and the rest of you."

Fee, Fergal. Andy, Anna, Mo, Gina and Bella all headed for the door. Izzy plonked herself on the cup tree and the rest of the fairies and elves found somewhere to sit. Danny had already placed the fairy table in the centre of Penny's table and cupped his hand so that Finn, who seemed to have attached himself to Danny, could have a comfortable seat. Izzy then began her story about all she had done and seen during the day. Long before she had finished the other fairies and elves had returned, the pizza was cooked and the fairy banquet was prepared.

Izzy continued to recount her adventures as everyone tucked into their meals. At the end of the story Penny was astonished to learn about all the woodland creatures and the ones residing in her garden unbeknown to her. She couldn't wait to meet Bertie and his wives and the deer and promised Izzy they would return to the clearing tomorrow evening after work.

It was decided that as the day after was Saturday Penny, Danny, Trixie, fairies and elves would go and explore the campsite that Danny had his lodge on and then Sunday they would go and visit the deer. Penny went to a drawer and pulled out a sheaf of photos and proceeded to show the fairies and elves what a human hotel and holiday park looked like and all the fairies and elves felt they could create something similar on the island.

Finn and Fergal proceeded to explain that they would like to convert a tree stump into their permanent residence and that Topaz had already secured the woodpecker's services to hollow out some holes for them high up on the stump so that their home didn't get flooded.

Danny and Penny suggested that they helped the fairies to raise the island so that the hotel and holiday homes didn't flood either. Penny suggested they made the hotel from a tree stump so it blended in with the surroundings and Danny suggested they use smaller logs and tree stumps to form the holiday lodges. By the time everyone had finished eating all the team had a clear vision of how Penny's Kingdom would evolve and were excited at the prospect of how their respective skills could contribute.

Suddenly Izzy looked up.

"Oh my goodness the sun has about gone so I think we need to head outside and get this meeting started," wailed Izzy.

"Don't panic Izzy," Mercury soothed her. "You know that fairies and elves don't bother about time and the birds and animals are all at home so it doesn't matter how late this meeting is. Once everyone hears exactly how much work you have already done today they will be in awe of you and be happy to help. Come on Penny and Danny, you two have also a large part to play in the creation of Penny's Kingdom."

Penny, Danny and their team of fairies and elves emerged from the house headed by Queen Izzy. They were all immediately escorted by a teaming gaggle of fairies and elves who had prepared a makeshift stage for Izzy to address her subjects between two tree stumps. The workers had intended the smaller tree stump to be used by Izzy's deputies but when they saw another human, who appeared to be totally accepted and at ease with their queen, they quickly found four extra seats to put on the stage to flank their queen.

Izzy took up her position and a hush descended on the crowd.

"Welcome to you all. Before I start this meeting properly I would like to introduce you to my two human friends Penny and Danny. We know that Penny can talk and hear animals, fairies and elves and Danny has been communicating all evening with us fairies and elves so I imagine he is like Penny, one of our special humans, but we will check at the end of the meeting. I also want to introduce you to my now extended team. Most of you already know Mercury, Emerald, Sapphire and Topaz who are my deputies but I have now added to the team to assist me in developing Penny's Kingdom. Our aim is to make it the best fairy kingdom in the country, if not the world, and to do that there will be a huge amount of work and changes to make to both this, our proposed new kingdom headquarters, and the area surrounding the waterfall. We have now got four new areas of expertise headed by experts in their fields who will oversee the work needed to ensure Penny's Kingdom is the best we can make it. I will now, in turn, introduce you to them and they will explain what their team will be engaged in. First we have Gina and Bella. They will head our catering team. Okay over to you girls."

"Hi everyone, as our name suggests, we will be involved in ensuring there is enough food stored in our communal larders to feed you all and any visitors who stay or pass through our kingdom. We will work closely with other team members to gather or plant food accordingly."

A huge cheer went up and several voices could be heard saying how delighted they were to have a catering team. Izzy took over the floor again.

"Well you all seem to be in agreement with that decision. Next we have Mimi and Mo who will be in charge of all the lighting in the kingdom. There will be lighting in and around the kingdom headquarters, in your own private permanent residences if you want it, around the waterfall so it is lit up even when the moon is covered by clouds and the new visitor accommodation we are going to build, so that you resident fairies and elves do not have to give up or share your homes when we have visitors."

Mimi and Mo stepped forward shyly.

"Hello we are pleased to serve our queen in any way we can, but feel the most important job is to get our new kingdom headquarters flooded with light. Mo and I will no doubt need your help from time to time and are happy and willing to listen to suggestions from you."

Another huge cheer erupted from the garden. Penny thought it was a good job that she hadn't any neighbours and that by now it was too dark for any dog walkers to be out. Again Izzy moved to the centre of the platform.

"Like Mimi said any suggestions please come forward both over the next few days and anytime in the future. My next pair I am calling, is my interior team, who will be responsible for ensuring we have enough insulation for our permanent homes once Penny, and maybe helped by Danny, has found old pots, pans, kettle, teapots etc. to place around the garden for you all to choose your own home. I know, at present, many of you sleep in and around the garden under stones, in flowers etc. but none of these places will be very warm and dry in winter hence we are providing you all with alternatives. Finn and Fergal here will be collecting wool, leaves for drying, dandelion fluff and anything else they feel will be suitable for the interiors of your homes. Once we have the visitor accommodation built they will be maintaining all that too. They will help the catering team by gathering anything they need on their travels. Anything I have missed boys?"

"I don't think so Queen Izzy, Fergal and me will be living over near the visitor accommodation. We are then on hand if any of our visitors need anything and we will build plenty of storage sheds so we can store wool, leaves and other provisions for use when those items are in short supply."

"Finn, it might be a good idea to add extra storage to your site so we can keep or surplus food stuff in the same place," suggested Gina.

"Of course Fergal and I will be happy to provide extra storage places for all the things we collect if you want Gina," replied Finn.

"You see how already our heads are communicating and working together to make this kingdom great," Izzy said when she returned to her position on the stage. "Lastly we have formed a 'ground staff' team. This team is responsible for ensuring all our grounds are maintained, kept clean and tidy, but that doesn't mean all the work is left to them, developing the headquarters by planting seeds, trees and plants to grow food, shelter and anything else the kingdom needs. Yes, we can forage, in the forest as Finn and Fergal will be doing, but in the middle of winter this will be impossible. So I have appointed Anna, Andy and Fee to do this valuable task. As a team they work well together but also have individual skills that they will bring to the team. They will work closely with the other team heads, Finn and Fergal to collect seeds and plants, Mimi and Mo to ensure adequate lighting without interfering with your privacy and Gina and Bella to make sure they plant the resources the catering team need. Once the visitor accommodation is built then this team will take over the landscaping of the site to ensure it looks beautiful so our visitors will return again and again. So everyone, that is your management team. Now a quick outline of our proposed plans although many of these are mere ideas and will evolve as time moves on. Whilst exploring this morning I found a gorgeous dry cave behind the waterfall with a beautiful staircase leading up to it. I want to make the cave into a banqueting hall/ballroom for when we have visiting dignitaries from other fairy kingdoms. Mimi has the job of sorting the lighting and then we will need the interior designing. We will need tables and chairs and a stage for the band to sit on. Mimi will sort out lighting for the staircase too. The staircase joins the stream that is the overflow for the pool at the base of the waterfall. If you follow the stream it eventually joins the other stream that flows from the forest behind Penny's summer house. We have water voles making homes in this bank. Are you here water voles?"

A huge shout of "Yes we are all here Queen Izzy" greeted this question.

"Good I am pleased you have all come. To go back to my, sorry no, our plans, where all the streams meet we have a lovely little island where we propose to build a fairy hotel and fairy holiday lodges to accommodate all our visitors from other kingdoms. Now, I know none of you know what a hotel or lodge looks like, and neither did I until earlier tonight, but Penny had some photographs of human hotels and lodges which helped us with ideas. Also Danny actually owns a lodge, and he is sure that in the forest where he stays are several fairy hotels, so the day after tomorrow he is taking us there to explore. I will update you once we know more. Mercury, Emerald, Sapphire and Topaz will be taking up residence in Penny's summer house, sorry Penny I forgot to mention that to you, eventually, once we get them a fairy door installed. That way you can access them easily when necessary. I think I will continue to live in Penny's cottage especially as I seem to be straddling the fairy world, where we sleep all day and work at night, and the human world who do the opposite. Some animals like mice and hedgehogs follow the fairy world, others like deer and goats the human world so to ensure I remain available to all my subjects I will straddle both. We will continue to develop the plans for our first ball in about four weeks which is to be held on the Summer Solstice or we call it Midsummer Night that Mercury and the team had begun to design. This will be just our kingdom fairies and elves but in the autumn we will invite other fairies and elves to join us at our Autumn Ball. Finally we are planning to hold a full National Ball here in winter and we hope we can make it a yearly event and host the very first Winter National Fairy Ball ever. At the moment I am unsure how much, if at all, our plans will affect you all who live in and around Penny's garden, and what will be our headquarters, but I hope this meeting has cleared up some of your questions. Thank you for taking time out from your busy lives."

Izzy stepped down from her platform followed by her deputies and her operational heads. Suddenly there was a crescendo of voices raised in 'She's a jolly good fellow' and then 'God Save the Queen' before all the many elves and fairies dispersed. The hedgehogs and mice briefly came to make Penny and Danny's acquaintance and to everyone's delight Danny could also communicate with animals. Penny promised the hedgehogs that she would give some thought to names for the new babies of both Hetty and the new hedgehog mum and that she was honoured and pleased to meet both the mice and water voles although as she said she probably wouldn't see much of the water voles as they were not technically living in her garden. As the garden slowly emptied and Penny and Danny wandered back to the house Izzy briefly returned to her platform and surveyed her kingdom. With a contented sigh she relived her day and wondered what adventures awaited her tomorrow and the rest of the future. Whatever she encountered from now on she was sure nothing would compare to this, her first day as Fairy Queen of Penny's Kingdom.

Lightning Source UK Ltd.
Milton Keynes UK
UKOW04f2347191017
311284UK00001B/151/P